A Note from [Gorgeous]

Did you ever meet a guy you just knew was The One? That happened to me not long ago. I had the hugest crush on the new boy next door—only he sort of had a crush on someone else. . . .

I guess you're dying to hear all about it, but first I want to explain something.

I come from a *very* large family.

Right now there are nine people and a dog living in our house—and for all I know, someone new could move in at any time. There's me, my big sister, D.J., my little sister, Michelle, and my dad, Danny. But that's just the beginning.

Uncle Jesse came first. My dad asked him to come live with us when my mom died, to help take care of me and my sisters.

Back then, Uncle Jesse didn't know much about taking care of three little girls. He was more into rock 'n' roll. So Dad asked his old college buddy, Joey Gladstone, to help out. Joey didn't know anything about kids, either—but it sure was funny watching him learn!

Having Uncle Jesse and Joey around was like having three dads instead of one! But then something even better happened—Uncle Jesse fell in love. He married Becky Donaldson, Dad's co-host on his TV show, *Wake Up, San Francisco*. Aunt Becky's so nice—she's more like a big sister than an aunt.

Next Uncle Jesse and Aunt Becky had twin baby boys. Their names are Nicky and Alex, and they are adorable!

I love being part of a big family. Still, things can get pretty crazy when you live in such a full house!

FULL HOUSE™
Stephanie

The Boy-Oh-Boy Next Door

Rita Miami

A Parachute Press Book

A MINSTREL® BOOK

PUBLISHED BY POCKET BOOKS

New York   London   Toronto   Sydney   Tokyo   Singapore

This book is a work of fiction. Names, characters, places, and incidents are either products of the author's imagination or are used fictitiously. Any resemblance to actual events or locales or persons, living or dead, is entirely coincidental.

A MINSTREL PAPERBACK *ORIGINAL*

 A Minstrel Book published by
POCKET BOOKS, a division of Simon & Schuster Inc.
1230 Avenue of the Americas, New York, NY 10020

A Parachute Press Book
Copyright © 1993 by Lorimar Television, Inc.

FULL HOUSE, characters, names and all related indicia are trademarks of Lorimar Television © 1993.

ISBN: 0-671-88121-3

First Minstrel Books printing December 1993

10 9 8 7 6 5 4 3 2 1

A MINSTREL BOOK and colophon are registered trademarks of Simon & Schuster Inc.

Cover photo: Schultz Photography

Printed in the U.S.A.

The Boy-Oh-Boy Next Door

CHAPTER
1

◆ ◀ ◆ ◆

"Okay, I'll hang on." Stephanie Tanner switched the cordless phone to her right ear and flipped off her shoes. Lifting her feet up onto the couch, she settled in among the pillows for a nice, long Friday afternoon chat.

"Hey, Steph," called Joey, coming into the living room from his room downstairs. "Any chance of the phone being free anytime in the next, oh, say, six months?"

Stephanie put her hand over the mouthpiece. "I'm on hold," she whispered. "Allie's parents gave her three-way calling for her birthday, and I'm waiting while she dials Darcy. If it works, then all three of us can talk at once."

Joey Gladstone sighed. He'd moved into the Tanner household several years before to help Danny Tanner after Danny's wife, Pam, had been killed in a car accident, leaving him with three small daughters to raise. Pam's brother Jesse, his wife, Becky, and their two-year-old twins, Nicky and Alex, lived upstairs in what had once been the attic.

"Guess maybe I should go hunt for a pay phone, huh?" said Joey.

"Oh, Joey . . . Allie? Yeah, I'm still here. Darcy, is that you? Hey, Allie! It works! Three-way calling is so cool!" crooned Stephanie, twisting a lock of her blond hair around her finger.

"There's probably a pay phone within a few blocks," said Joey. "Or a few miles."

"A clothes swap? Right, right."

"Don't worry about me," Joey said as he headed for the front door. "If I'm not back in time for dinner, just keep mine warm in the oven." But at the front door, Joey stopped and turned around. "On second thought, maybe I'll just have a little snack now and hope that by the time I finish, the phone might be free." He turned and walked into the kitchen.

"One of these Saturdays," said Stephanie, "let's do it. I'm sick of just about everything in my clos— Whoa! Hold it a sec. Hey!" Stephanie gave the big golden retriever who had sprung up beside her a gentle push back onto the floor. "You know you're not allowed up on the couch. No, no, not you, Darcy. I was talking to Comet. Phew! You don't smell too great. No, not *you*, Allie. The dog! Now, where were we? What, Darcy? No way! Red is your color. Trust me, you'll look as fabulous as Whitney Houston did at the Grammys. She had on this totally bright red outfit. . . ."

Stephanie was so absorbed in discussing the clothes exchange that she didn't see her father, Danny Tanner, come into the living room. She never noticed him until he was standing at the foot of the couch, right beside Comet, looking down at her with his have-I-got-a-job-for-you smile.

"Hold it, guys." Stephanie covered the mouthpiece with her palm once again and returned her father's look. "Yes?"

"Didn't you just tell me," Danny said, "that you couldn't give Comet a bath because you had to start writing your story for the Golden Gate Creative Writing Contest?"

"Uh . . . yes, I did," Stephanie admitted. "And what I'm doing at the moment may look to you like talking on the phone, but actually, I'm doing some very important research for my story." She took her hand away from the mouthpiece. "Now, Allie, could you please repeat just what kind of main characters you most enjoy reading about?"

"Well," said her father, "if you don't clean up this dog's act sometime this weekend, you'll be able to write a new story, from personal experience, called 'Grounded.' "

"I hear you," said Stephanie.

"By the way, Steph, are you using the phone for vital communication?" her dad asked. "Or are you going for a new longest-call world's record?"

Stephanie did not dignify these questions by answering them. Instead, she sighed deeply and waited until her father left the room.

"So," Stephanie said to her friends, "back to switching clothes. Who wants my turquoise T-shirt with the black rose on it?"

"I do," said seven-year-old Michelle, the youngest Tanner sister, who was now standing in the spot their father had just occupied. "And you can have my T-shirt with the baby whale."

4

"Michelle!" Stephanie jumped up from the couch. "I don't want your disgusting sea-life T-shirt! Can't you see I'm talking to Darcy and Allie?"

"No," said Michelle. "I can only see you."

"Ooooh," Stephanie groaned. "I have no privacy at . . ." Suddenly, Stephanie glanced out the living-room window and caught a glimpse of an unfamiliar patch of red. "Hey, that's a moving van. What's it doing in front of our house?" Still clutching the phone, she walked over to the large bay window for a closer look.

"It's for next door," said Michelle, coming to join Stephanie at the window. "Our new neighbors are moving in."

"This could be good," Stephanie reported to her friends. "I wonder what kind of stuff our new neighbors have. What, Darcy? Yeah, don't I wish. But you know what the chances are of an extremely cute boy, in seventh, maybe eighth grade, moving in—zilch."

"Maybe it's a cute second-grade boy," said Michelle.

"You're too young for a boyfriend," Stephanie told her sister.

"So are you," said Michelle.

"No, I'm not. I'm eleven, just the age D.J. was when she got her first crush on a boy."

Michelle's eyes opened wide. "D.J. crushed a boy?"

"Reality check, Michelle. It means she *liked* a boy, okay?" Stephanie turned her attention back to her phone buddies. "I guess it *could* be a boy moving in. And if it *is* a boy, then he'd be the boy next door."

Stephanie liked the sound of that—the boy next door. It sounded, well, sort of romantic. But not too romantic. Just right, actually, for a first boyfriend. "Oh, sorry, Allie. What'd you say? Okay, I will, but nothing that interesting is being unloaded. Just some cardboard boxes. Lots of boxes. And here comes what looks like a dining-room table. Not too exciting—but hold it! Two movers are now carrying a . . . a basketball backboard and hoop! They're going up the steps. This is very professional-looking equipment."

"And they've got a dog," said Michelle. "A *big* dog."

"I think you're right," said Stephanie, "unless the large doghouse that is now being carried to the side of the house is actually a guest room.

And now we have a pair of stereo speakers covered with bubble wrap. Okay, sports and music fans, we think we like our new neigh— Hey, a red Jeep's pulling up right behind the van."

Stephanie held her breath. Did that red Jeep hold the boy next door? The car door cracked slightly and then opened wide as a large furry dog bounded out, followed by a slim, dark-haired woman trying to hold on to the dog's leash.

"So far, we have the dog next door," Stephanie told Darcy and Allie. "It's that kind that wears a keg of brandy around its neck and rescues lost skiers. Right, a Saint Bernard. And I believe the person getting dragged up the steps after the dog is the mom next door, and the dad next door is getting out of the other side of the car and . . . I don't believe it."

Stephanie stood still as a statue, while the phone slid ever so slowly from her hand.

Michelle caught it on its way to the floor and put it to her ear. "Hello, Darcy? Allie? This is Michelle. Stephanie is still here, only she's staring out the window. What? Oh, nothing much. All I see is some boy coming up the front steps . . . Okay." Michelle tugged at her sister's sleeve. "Earth to Stephanie," she said, holding up the phone. "It's for you."

"You guys won't believe this," Stephanie told her friends. "The boy next door is . . . beyond good-looking. I mean, we're talking movie star. Wait! There he goes, down the stairs again. Not only is he totally cute, but he is also totally helpful. Okay, okay. He's got dark hair, not too short, not too long. A red-and-black plaid shirt, slightly faded jeans. Nice tan, nothing overboard, just healthy-looking. Eyes . . . maybe brown; it's hard to tell from this distance." Stephanie turned to her sister. "Michelle, you know where Joey keeps his binoculars?"

"Why?" Michelle asked. "Are you going to spy on the new boy?"

"Not spy, exactly," said Stephanie. "Just get a closer look. Wait a minute, guys," she said into the phone.

For a moment Stephanie simply stared out the window, ignoring the frantic voices coming out of the phone, saying "What? What? What?" At last she croaked, "It's D.J.! My big sister's down on the sidewalk, talking to the people next door, and mostly to the boy next door!" Stephanie pressed her nose to the windowpane, trying to get closer to see more. "I can't tell what they're talking about. Now D.J.'s waving good-bye to him. Here she comes, up our steps."

Handing the phone over to Michelle, Stephanie ran to open the front door.

"Stephanie will be right back," Michelle told Darcy and Allie. "In the meantime, here's what's happening." She held the phone out so that the girls could hear what was going on across the room.

Stephanie practically yanked D.J. inside the house, closing the door behind her.

"Hey!" D.J. exclaimed. "What's going on?"

"Nothing, nothing." Stephanie tried not to appear too excited. "So, uh, what's the new family like?"

"Well, they're the Schwabs. Joyce and Art Schwab. Joyce has a job with the museum down on—"

"Skip Joyce and Art," said Stephanie. "Get to the son."

"Eddie?"

"Eddie," Stephanie sighed, collapsing onto the couch. "That's the one."

"All I know," said D.J., putting down her

books and then sitting on the couch herself, "is that the Schwabs moved here from Los Angeles. Eddie seems like a nice guy. He's got a dog named Max; he likes to play basketball and is interested in writing. I think that's it. Oh, yeah, and he's in ninth grade."

Stephanie's face fell. "Ninth grade!"

"That's the whole report for now." D.J. stood, scooped up her books, and headed for the stairs. "I've got major cramming to do for my statistics exam on Monday and this is about the only free time I've got. See you later."

"You can have Stephanie back now," Michelle said into the phone before handing it to her sister.

"His name's Eddie," Stephanie said into the phone. "Isn't Eddie a beautiful name?"

"What about Max?" Michelle asked. "Do you think Max is a beautiful name too?"

Stephanie nodded at her sister. "I am in love with Eddie Schwab," she announced. "But he's in ninth grade. He'd never be interested in a sixth grader. No way! What do you think, Allie?" Glumly, Stephanie listened for a moment, nodding in agreement. "That's what I think too. It's hopeless."

"Do you think Max is a more beautiful name for a dog than Comet?" Michelle asked.

"Shh, Michelle. I can't hear Darcy." As Stephanie listened to her other friend, she brightened. "Really? You think he might?"

"What'd she say?" Michelle asked.

"She said, 'Go for it, girl!' " Stephanie whispered to her sister. Getting up and going to the window again, she added, "Thanks, Darcy! You know, I think I will see if I can't make a big impression on the boy next door. After all, what have I got to lose?"

"Your life," said Joey, coming out of the kitchen, "if you don't get off the phone."

Stephanie sighed. "I have to go," she told her friends. "Call me later, Allie. Maybe *then* we can have a decent conversation."

CHAPTER
2

◆ ◂ ◆ ◆

Stephanie sat at her desk, which she'd converted into a dressing table, and looked into the mirror. Her long, straight blond hair, just shampooed, was behaving nicely. She was glad she'd decided to sneak up to the attic to raid her uncle Jesse's hair-care center. She'd just have to remember to return his special cream rinse right away, that was all. Earrings? Not too fancy, not too boring. Just right. A little of D.J.'s blush. First the right cheek, then the left.

On the other side of the room that the sisters shared, Michelle sat up in bed, her sleepy eyes staring at her sister in disbelief. "Stephanie?" she said. "What are you doing up before me on a Saturday morning?"

"Oh, just getting dressed," Stephanie chirped.

"Are you going out to breakfast or something?"

"Nope." Stephanie twisted up D.J.'s bright pink lipstick.

Michelle tossed off her covers and climbed out of bed. Comet, who had been lying beside the bed, rose to his feet and padded after Michelle over to the dressing table.

Michelle asked, "Are you having your picture taken?"

Stephanie shook her head.

"Getting ready for a party?"

Stephanie sighed and stood up. She was wearing her newest T-shirt, the one with an image of the Golden Gate Bridge done in gold glitter paint, and her new denim miniskirt.

"How come you're so dressed up?"

"Get used to it, Michelle," said Stephanie. "I'm turning over a new leaf."

"I don't see any leaf."

"That's just a way of saying that I'm starting over," Stephanie explained as she slipped her feet into her brand-new blue suede flats. "You see, I've decided that my own family, the people I love most in all the world, deserve to see me looking my best."

13

Michelle wrinkled up her forehead. "You're getting this dressed up for me and D.J.?"

"And for Dad and Joey and Uncle Jesse," said Stephanie. "And Becky and Nicky and Alex."

Michelle looked as if she didn't entirely believe what her sister was saying.

"Stand back," Stephanie ordered as she picked up a green-glass perfume bottle from her dressing table.

"What's that?" Michelle asked.

"True Love," Stephanie answered, taking off the cap. "I read in a magazine how this is the way to put on just the right amount of perfume." With that, she raised the bottle to shoulder level, pressed the top, and sprayed a good-size cloud of True Love into the air in front of her. Then, closing her eyes, she stepped into the mist.

As the droplets settled, Comet shook his head, gave a loud sneeze, and galloped from the room.

"Phew!" Michelle waved her hand in front of her nose.

"Not only am I going to look and smell my best," Stephanie continued, "I'm also going to be my best."

"Are you turning into another leaf?" Michelle asked.

"*Over* a new leaf," her sister corrected. "I want to contribute something to our family. I want to help with all the work that needs to be done to keep this household running. I want to pitch in and help with the chores. I'm going to . . .

". . . be very busy," said Michelle.

After a final check in the mirror, Stephanie walked to the door. "I'm going out to cut the grass," she said, and then held up a hand. "No, don't thank me. It's the least I can do to give back to my family all that they have given me." She quickly glanced out the window at the boy next door, who was in his yard fiddling with a lawn mower.

As Stephanie swept out of the room, Michelle looked confused. With a shrug she said, "Maybe cutting the grass means something else, like turning over a leaf."

The Tanners' lawn mower sat in a corner of their garage, looking larger and more complicated than Stephanie remembered. Not that she really remembered very much about it, having done her best to avoid anything remotely connected with lawns and yard work all her life. Still, as she stood in the garage now, she wished she'd paid a little more attention when she'd watched her father show D.J. how it worked. She had to pull hard on the black handle down by the wheels, that much she knew. And if she pulled hard enough, the motor would start. Okay. Propping one blue suede shoe on top of the mower, Stephanie mentally chanted *Ready, set, go!*—and yanked the handle as hard as she could.

The mower answered with a pitiful cough.

Stephanie pulled again.

This time the mower sputtered a bit before it grew silent.

"You can do this, Stephanie Tanner," she said to herself, and gave a mighty tug.

ROAR! The mower sprang to life.

Keeping a firm grip, Stephanie pushed the mower forward, out of the garage. For a moment, the bright sunlight blocked out everything. But after blinking a couple of times, Stephanie's eyes adjusted—just in time for her to see that she was heading into the pansy bed. Quickly, after decapitating only a few flowery heads, she steered the mower to the right. Uh-oh, that was *too* far to the right. She jerked the mower to the left. This wasn't all that easy. A quick glance to the rear confirmed that she was making a very jagged path across the grass. *Oh, well,* she thought, *I can always mow over this area again, when I've had a little more practice.*

Stephanie managed to hold her mower fairly steady as she edged over toward the tall hedge that separated the Tanners' yard from the Schwabs' yard. *Stupid hedge,* Stephanie thought. How was Eddie going to notice her if he couldn't even see her? Maybe she should get a little closer, and then at the gap in the hedge she could . . . Yikes! The mower thumped over a bump and veered directly into the dark, lumpy soil beneath the hedge. Stephanie pulled on the mower, trying to back it up, but its wheels simply spun, digging the mower deeper into the dirt. And then, to make matters worse, the mower belched out a cloud of thick black smoke, shuddered, and died.

Wishing that she could do the same, Stephanie stood in the trench, still gripping the lifeless mower. Her new blue shoes, she saw, were now coated with clots of damp dirt. Dirt had spattered the fronts of her legs up past her knees.

"Need some help?" came a voice from the opposite side of the hedge.

Stephanie's mind whirled. Quickly she bent over and brushed the soil from her legs, her socks, her shoes. "Oh, no, not really," she answered. Then, abandoning her mower, she hurried to the gap in the hedge. Stepping through it and into the Schwabs' yard, she walked over to where the boy next door stood, behind an old-fashioned no-motor mower.

"Never try to mow a hedge," she said.

The boy next door laughed.

"I'm Stephanie Tanner," she said. "The, uh, girl next door."

"Hi, I'm Eddie Schwab. I guess that makes me the boy next door."

"So," said Stephanie, "you just moved in and here you are, cutting the grass already?"

"It was more my father's idea than mine," Eddie admitted. "But I don't mind mowing the lawn that much. At least not with this mower." He gave one of its wheels a little tap with his sneaker. "It's a little harder to push than a power mower, maybe, but I like the fact that I'm not using any gas or causing any pollution."

"That is so . . . Earth sensitive," said Stephanie.

Eddie shrugged. "Every little bit helps."

"I've got to talk to my father about our gas-hog of a lawn mower." Stephanie rolled her eyes. "Really, it's time we traded it in for one like yours."

Chatting with Eddie was a breeze, Stephanie thought. And it wasn't as if they were talking about silly, shallow things, either. They were talking about ways to save the planet!

"Well," said Eddie, "I guess I'd better finish up."

"Right, right," said Stephanie, her mind spinning in hopes of finding a way to keep the conversation going. "Me too. Really. I was wondering, after your grass is all cut and everything, if you'd like to come over to our house and, you know, meet everybody."

Eddie looked interested. "I've already met one other girl next door," he said. "Your sister D.J. What do the initials D.J. stand for, anyway? Disc jockey?"

"Donna Jo," said Stephanie quickly. "Anyway, sometimes on Saturdays we have chili for lunch and . . ."

19

"Well, I'll come over," said Eddie, "but I gave up eating meat a year or so ago."

"Oh, you're a vegetarian," Stephanie said. "Well, that's really amazing because . . . I am too." *At least*, she added silently, *I am now.*

"But you eat chili?"

"I guess I'm so used to, you know, being a vegetarian that I forgot to say it was vegetarian chili. I mean, what other kind would a vegetarian such as myself be talking about? It's really delicious. . . ."

Stephanie closed her eyes and thought back to last week when—lucky break!—she'd helped Joey with his special recipe for the very dish they were discussing. There was, she knew, a container of vegetarian chili in their freezer. "It's made with beans, red and green peppers, chopped onion, tomatoes, black olives, a little basil, oregano, salt, pepper, and the secret ingredient—corn. It's served over rice and topped with fresh tomato bits, avocado, and broken-up taco shells."

"Wow," said Eddie. "That does sound good. You made that recipe up?"

"Oh," said Stephanie, "I guess you could say that." Or, she thought, you *could* say Joey had made it up. But his chili hadn't included the taco shell topping. She'd added that. So, she could honestly say that it was her recipe— couldn't she?

"Well, I'll have to try to make your chili one of these days," said Eddie. "And maybe you and . . . and D.J. can come over and see how I did."

"I think that could be arranged," said Stephanie.

"Hi, guys!"

Stephanie turned and saw D.J. coming up Eddie's driveway.

"Hey, it's D.J.!" said Eddie.

"D.J.!" Stephanie exclaimed. "What are *you* doing here?"

"I told our new neighbor that I'd give him a tour of the number-one point of local interest— the mall," she said. "So, Eddie, should we go?"

Eddie checked his watch. "How did it get to be ten o'clock so fast?" He looked up and grinned at D.J. "The grass will have to wait, I guess," he said, wheeling his mower around and pushing it toward the garage. "Give me two minutes, D.J."

When Eddie was out of earshot, D.J. turned

21

to Stephanie. "I'd ask you to come with us," she said, "but I've got to get back for my prom committee meeting, so this is going to be the world's quickest mall tour. I don't really have time to wait while you change."

"Change?" Stephanie echoed. "Oh, you mean my shoes?"

"Well . . ." said D.J.

Stephanie looked down and noticed for the first time that the spinning wheels of the power mower had done more damage than she had realized. Her skirt and even her once-white T-shirt were now dusted with dirt.

Eddie walked back over to D.J. "Ready when you are," he said. "See you, Stephanie."

It took an effort for Stephanie to raise her arm to wave good-bye. She stood where she was, watching her sister and the boy next door as they walked away.

Slowly, Stephanie trudged back through the break in the hedge to her own yard. And there, beside the mower where it had plowed into the hedge, stood her father.

"Steph?" said Danny. "Do you know anything about how this got here?"

Stephanie took a deep breath. "As a matter

of fact," she said, "I do." And she explained how she had been trying to help with the family chores by mowing the lawn. "But," she finished up, "I kind of got stuck in the mud."

"No problem," said her father as he tugged the mower back onto the grass. "And I appreciate your family spirit so much that I'd like to invite you to go out for a pizza with Michelle and me."

Stephanie smiled. "Sure," she said. "But isn't it a little early for pizza?"

Her father nodded. "I was talking about later," he said, "after you finish cutting the grass."

CHAPTER
3

♦ ◀ ♦ ♦

Danny, Joey, Uncle Jesse, Becky, the twins, D.J., and Michelle were already seated at the Tanner dinner table that night when Stephanie pulled out her chair and sat down.

"Sorry if I kept everyone waiting," she said glumly. "You could have started without me."

"We wouldn't start without—" her father began, and then he exclaimed, "Stephanie! Your hands! What happened?"

"Oh, these?" Stephanie raised her hands, each of which was wrapped in a grotesque combination of Band-Aids, gauze pads, and adhesive tape. "I was just trying to protect my

24

blisters," she said in a pitiful voice, "before they got infected."

"Blisters?" said D.J. "How did you get blisters?"

"From holding a hot telephone, maybe?" Joey suggested.

"From the lawn mower," said Stephanie. "But they'll probably be healed in a week or two."

"After dinner, I'll take a look at them," said her father. "In the meantime, let's eat."

The adults' conversation centered on plans for the following day, Sunday, when Vicki, the woman Danny Tanner was engaged to, would be flying in for a visit from her home in Chicago.

"I say we all take in a baseball game," said Joey. "Could somebody please pass the meat loaf?"

"Here you go, Joey," said Danny. "How about you, Steph? Can I put a slice of meat loaf on your plate?"

"No, thank you," said Stephanie. "I don't really eat meat."

"Since when?" asked Jesse.

"I've been a vegetarian for quite a while," Stephanie replied. After all, it had been eight hours since her conversation with Eddie.

"Well, have lots of broccoli, then," said Jesse. "It's great for the hair." He ran a hand through his own thick black mane and added, "By the way, has anyone seen my cream rinse? I can't find it anywhere."

Stephanie made a mental note to return it right after dinner.

"You know, Joey," Jesse continued, "I'm not wild about the idea of a baseball game tomorrow. Why don't we take Vicki to a nice lunch? Somewhere outdoors, with a great view of the bay and the Golden Gate Bridge?"

"Speaking of Golden Gate, Steph," said Danny, "have you gotten a start on that story for the Golden Gate Creative Writing Contest?"

"Sort of," said Stephanie.

"How do you 'sort of' start on a story?" her father wanted to know.

"I mean, my mind is hard at work on it, but it may be a while"—she held up her bandaged hands—"before I get anything down on paper."

"You want to borrow my tape recorder?" Joey asked as he helped himself to another serving of rice. "You could talk your story into it."

Stephanie sighed. "Thanks, Joey. I'll think about it."

After dinner, it was D.J. and Stephanie's turn to put the dishes in the dishwasher.

"Why don't you just keep me company, Steph? I'll do the dishes," D.J. suggested. "Because of your blisters and all."

"Thanks!" Stephanie perched herself on a stool at the counter opposite the sink.

"Listen," D.J. said, "is anything the matter?"

"Not really," said Stephanie. "I've gotten used to the constant pain in my hands now." She picked at the edge of a piece of tape on her left hand. "How was your tour of the mall?"

"It was okay," said D.J. "Eddie bought Max a new water dish at Pet Palace."

"Oh," said Stephanie as she unwound the tape from her left hand and flexed her fingers. "So have you told Steve yet?"

"Told him what?"

"That you're breaking up with him."

"Why would I tell him that?" asked D.J.

"Well, I thought maybe you asked Eddie to

go to the mall because you were, you know, interested in him."

"Oh, right! Just what I need during my senior year in high school—a ninth-grade boyfriend!" D.J. laughed.

Stephanie had to laugh too. It *was* a crazy idea.

D.J. added, "I had to go over to the mall this morning anyway, so, just to be friendly, I asked Eddie if he wanted to come along. He's a nice guy, but, you know, the main men in my life are Steve, Steve, and Steve."

"Well, that's good," said Stephanie, pulling the wrappings from her right hand. "Boy, is that ever good."

Coming into the kitchen with a stack of dirty plates, Danny caught a look at his daughter's hands. "Stephanie, it looks to me as if those blisters are, uh, healing pretty quickly."

"They are, Dad," she said. "Good thing I wrapped them up like that, isn't it?"

"The pain's all gone?" asked D.J.

"Totally."

"Then here." D.J. handed her sister a soapy sponge. "You can wipe the table and the counters."

Stephanie was just wringing out the sponge when the doorbell rang. She heard the door open and D.J. say, "Oh, hi, Eddie. Come on in and meet everyone."

Quickly, Stephanie checked her hair in the reflection in a glass cabinet door. She could hear Eddie saying how nice it was to meet Danny, Jesse, Becky, and Michelle. Then she heard him say, "D.J., do you think I could borrow a hammer?"

Stephanie chose this moment to make her entrance into the living room. "Hi, Eddie," she said. "Did I hear you say you're looking for a hammer?"

Eddie nodded. "We've got one—somewhere—but I couldn't find the box it's packed in, and so . . . I came over here."

"Are you building something?" asked Stephanie. She could picture Eddie constructing a bench, maybe, to put out in the backyard; a bench just big enough for two. And at night, when it got very dark, he'd ask her to come out and sit beside him and gaze up at the stars and talk about how to save planet Earth.

"Not exactly," said Eddie. "I just want to hang a few pictures."

"Oh, so you like art?" asked Stephanie. "All the tools and stuff are downstairs. D.J., I know how much studying you have to do for that big statistics exam. Come on, Eddie, I'll take you down and help you look for a hammer." Leading the way to the stairs, she added, "I myself love art."

"I'm not sure you'd call what I'm hanging up art," Eddie said. "It's mostly photographs."

Stephanie could just imagine Eddie's room, its walls filled with gorgeous color photographs of Brazil's rain forest and whales and dolphins.

"The hammer's probably over this way," she said, leading the way to the tools. "So, are you mostly moved in?"

"Pretty much," said Eddie as he followed Stephanie over to the workbench. "My dad made sure the kitchen's all set, so at least we can eat. He's the big cook in our family."

"Boy, these tools are a mess," said Stephanie. "It could take forever to find a hammer," she added hopefully.

"Here's one," said Eddie. He reached into an open toolbox and lifted out a small, wooden-handled hammer.

"That's the kind you wanted?" said Stephanie. "I thought maybe something a little big-

30

ger, with more of a, you know, rubber grip on the end. Easier on the hands."

"It's not like I'm constructing a house or anything." Eddie smiled. "I think my hands won't be damaged too much from putting half a dozen nails into my wall."

"You're right," said Stephanie. "I don't know what I was thinking."

Eddie shifted the hammer to his other hand and started for the stairs. But then he turned back toward Stephanie. "You know something?" he said.

"What?"

"I know I just met you this morning and everything, but I feel like I've known you a lot longer."

Stephanie felt her face growing warm. "Like, how long? Like two days? Two months? Two years?"

Eddie's smile widened. "Oh, about two centuries," he said, and then he grew serious. "Have you ever moved?"

Stephanie shook her head. "People keep moving *into* this house," she said, "but we never move away."

"So you don't know what it's like to leave

all your friends and your room and everything familiar—even the *L.A. Times*."

"You're upset about leaving your old *newspaper*?"

"It sounds dumb, but you know how it is. You get used to one paper, and reading it every morning was something I looked forward to. Anyway, I've been dreading this move for months, ever since my dad broke the news about his new job." Eddie was quiet for a few seconds. "But," he went on, "then I met D.J. . . . and you too, of course," he added, "and I started to feel like I'd survive."

"You did?"

Eddie nodded. "I don't have a big family, like you do. And I felt really . . . alone. But then you showed up, and I didn't feel so bad anymore." Eddie smiled again, and then turned and went up the stairs.

In a haze of happiness, Stephanie followed and walked him to the door. "Don't hammer your thumb or anything," she said.

"I'll try not to," said Eddie.

"But if you do," said Stephanie, "come back over and borrow a Band-Aid."

*   *   *

Humming to herself, Stephanie drifted up the stairs. Breaking the rule about always knocking, she wafted into D.J.'s room and flopped down onto the bed. "I'm in love," she sighed.

D.J. put down her pencil. "Let me guess. Could it be with Eddie?"

"*E*-double *d-i-e*," Stephanie crooned. "Eddie is the boy for me! You know what he said? That he was really lonely when he moved here, but the minute he met me, he didn't feel lonely anymore."

"That's sweet." D.J. smiled at her younger sister. "And I'm sure it's true. You do have a way of making people feel good when they're around you."

Stephanie lay on her sister's bed, staring happily at the ceiling. Then suddenly she sat up, dismayed. "But as soon as he gets to school on Monday morning and meets a bunch of ninth-grade girls, he'll probably forget I'm alive."

"Oh, I don't know," said D.J. "There are lots of girls at the high school, but there's only one Stephanie Tanner."

"True." Stephanie smiled.

"And you know," continued D.J., "I think you and Eddie have many interests in common. That counts for a lot."

"Yeah?" asked Stephanie. "Such as?"

"Well, such as liking to write," said D.J. "Eddie told me that in L.A., he was co-editor of the school newspaper. He wants to be a journalist when he grows up. Maybe you should show him some of the stories you've written. What was that one that really cracked me up? I know—'The San Francisco Pickle Emergency.' "

"No way would I show that stupid story to Eddie!" Stephanie exclaimed.

"Why not? It was hilarious."

"That's just the problem," Stephanie explained. "I'm sure Eddie wrote all kinds of meaningful articles about important topics for his school paper. He'd think I was a twit if I showed him my stories." Stephanie made a face, and then grew thoughtful. "But maybe . . . maybe I could write something else, something I could use for the Golden Gate Writing Contest, that would show Eddie I can be the same kind of serious person he is."

"Just be yourself," said D.J. "The one and

only Stephanie Tanner. Now scram, so I can get some studying done before Steve comes over."

Her mind whirling with ideas, Stephanie went to her own bedroom, sat down at her desk, shoved over the bottles of perfume and makeup, and took out a sheet of notebook paper. On the top line she wrote her title:

Interview with a Dying Planet

CHAPTER
4

◆ ◀ ✦ ◆

"How do you spell *diseased organism*?" Stephanie asked.

"Dizzy organ what?" said Michelle.

"*Diseased organism*," Stephanie repeated without looking up from her notebook paper. She was seated at the kitchen counter, working on her seventh draft of "Interview with a Dying Planet" as she waited for her father to finish making his special Sunday brunch: waffles.

"*Diseased*," said Jesse, who sat beside Stephanie at the counter. "*D-i-s-e-a-s-e-d.*"

"*Organism,*" said Becky, straightening up from where she'd been squatting to supervise

36

Nicky and Alex as they patted Comet. "*O-r-g-a-n-i-s-m*. What are you writing, anyway, Steph?"

"My story for the Golden Gate Writing Contest," Stephanie replied. "How do you spell *corrupt society*?"

This time Joey spelled it for her, and then said, "Sounds like a pretty grim story."

"Can I help it if your generation has practically destroyed our world?" Stephanie answered. "How do you spell *polluted ecosystems*?"

"You need a dictionary," advised Joey, pouring himself another cup of coffee.

"Do you need to know how to spell *rabbit*?" asked Michelle. "It was on our spelling list last week. It's got two *b*'s."

"Thanks, Michelle." Stephanie worked on in silence while the adults continued the same discussion they'd had the evening before.

"Here's the movie section," said Becky, smoothing a page of the *San Francisco Dispatch* out on the counter. "It's perfect movie weather today, overcast and chilly. What about seeing *Lonely Hearts Are Crying*?"

"Vicki's seen it," said Danny. "Who wants the first waffle?"

"Me!" said Joey, snatching up the plate that

Danny offered. "And I'll take the second waffle and the third waffle too. Pass the syrup."

"Well, what about *The Big Itch*?" asked Becky.

"Not a chance." Danny put a waffle down in front of Stephanie. "Here you go, honey," he said. "One environmentally correct waffle. Eat up."

"Very funny," said Stephanie. "How do you know that the wheat in this waffle wasn't sprayed with deadly pesticides?" She put down her fork and wrote the phrase *deadly pesticides* on the margin of her paper.

Joey put his silverware down too. "You could make someone lose his appetite!" he said. Then, picking up his fork and knife again, he cut another bite of waffle. "Fortunately, almost nothing can make *me* lose *my* appetite."

"Steph, can I take a look at your composition?" asked Becky.

Stephanie passed her the paper, and Becky began to read aloud.

"Hello, this is Stephanie Tanner, anchorwoman for K.I.D. News. I'm here today to interview Planet Earth. So, Planet Earth, how are you?"

"I am sick, Stephanie. I am a horribly dis-eased organism."

"Why, that's awful, Planet Earth! What kinds of germs have caused this sickness?"

"Well, Stephanie, I'm glad you asked that. These deadly germs are none other than human beings. Yes, human beings who, like yourself, live in a horribly corrupt society that cares nothing for its own planet, the very source of its own life. It is society's carelessness that is wounding me, killing me."

"This is a very serious charge, Planet Earth. Can you give us some examples of how society is killing you?"

"Certainly, Stephanie. Why, did you know that America and other countries allow dumping of all sorts of poisonous chemicals, such as waste products from factories, into the ocean, killing fish and creating polluted ecosystems? Deadly pesticides are another major polluter of our globe, as are America's beastly gasoline-powered lawn mowers."

"Stephanie!" Danny interrupted Becky's reading. "Where did you get your facts? I hardly think that *lawn mowers* are any big deal when it comes to polluting the earth."

"Getting a push mower would help," Stephanie said. Then, quoting the boy next door, she added, "Every little bit helps." But when she took back her paper from Becky, she looked at it sheepishly. "It's not very good, is it?" she asked.

"I like the humans-as-germs bit," said Joey helpfully. "Like I always say at the beginning of my comedy act: 'Good evening, Ladies and Germs!'"

"Huh?" said Stephanie.

"Maybe you could put in something about how the planet was okay when Elvis was still alive," said Jesse.

Becky came over and put an arm around Stephanie's shoulders. "You know, Steph," she said, "this composition just doesn't sound like you. Is this *really* what you want to write about?"

Stephanie shrugged. "Not exactly," she admitted. "But I have to write about something important, something that matters."

"Don't writing teachers always say to write about what you know?" asked her father.

"But I don't know about anything important!"

Stephanie wailed. "My life is meaningless!" With that, she put her head down on her arms.

"Stephanie," said her dad, "how about coming to the airport with us to get Vicki? Then we'll all go do something fun. A movie might cheer you up. Or the baseball game."

Stephanie raised her head. "But that's just the problem!" she whined. "My life is already way too cheerful. I have to experience something deeper than just going to baseball games and movies. I have to do something important. And then I'll be able to write about it."

"Nothing's more important than a movie," said D.J., coming into the kitchen. "Especially a movie starring Tom Cruise." She bent down and picked up Nicky. Becky picked up Alex. "Hey, boys," D.J. said, "are you ready to rock 'n' roll with D.J. for a while?"

"You're sure you don't mind sitting this afternoon?" asked Becky.

"Not at all," said D.J. "I'll have time to study while they take a nap, and Steve can help me give them dinner when he comes over."

"I'll help her too," said Michelle.

"Thanks, Michelle. And maybe Stephanie will give you a hand," said Becky, going over to her middle niece and planting a kiss on the top of her head. "Steph, you're a terrific writer. When you decide what you really want to write, from your heart, you'll write something wonderful."

"Thanks, Becky," said Stephanie. "Thanks a lot."

"Sure you won't come with us, honey?" Danny asked.

Stephanie just shook her head.

"Well, as long as you have your heart set on staying here," said Danny, "maybe you'll find time to give Comet a bath."

After the grown-ups had left for the airport, Stephanie gathered all seven drafts of "Interview with a Dying Planet" and ripped each one into little pieces. She made a pile of the pieces and then called, "Alex! Nicky!" When the boys toddled over to where she sat, Stephanie said, "Hey, guys, it's snowing!" With that, she began sprinkling the little scraps down onto the floor. Nicky and Alex quickly got into the spirit of the snowstorm, twirling around and around as the paper pieces floated downward.

"Don't worry," Stephanie told D.J. "I'll clean it up." As she headed for the broom closet, she said, "What do you think I should do for the Golden Gate Writing Contest, D.J.?"

"I think Becky was right," said D.J. "You should write something from your heart, something that you really want to write."

As D.J. took the twins upstairs to put them down for their naps, Stephanie sat back down on the stool she'd occupied all morning long and straightened the pile of notebook paper in front of her. "What do I want to write about?" she asked herself, staring down at the empty top sheet of paper. "What is it that I, Stephanie Tanner, am dying to say?"

And suddenly she knew. Grabbing her pencil, she bent over and began writing something that she truly could write from her heart: *Dear Eddie*.

CHAPTER
5

◆ ◀ ◂ ◆

Sunday afternoon, Stephanie sat back on the living-room couch, once again holding the phone to her ear. "Allie? Yeah, I'm here. Darcy? Cool! Three-way calling strikes again!" She listened for a moment and then picked up a piece of notebook paper that was covered with writing, front and back. "Okay, guys," she said. "Just listen all the way through and then tell me if there's anything you think I should change—anything at all." Stephanie looked down at her paper and began to read aloud:

Dear Eddie,
    I never dreamed that someone like you would move in right next door to me and

change my life forever. Until I met you, no one knew the real me. Everyone thought I was just another kid. But you have changed all that. Now I am not afraid to show how truly intelligent and truly serious I truly am. You have given me the courage to be like, well, like really serious.

Last night, as I looked out my window into your window (I mean, not really *into* your window, because, you know, your shades were down. I am not a peeper!), I thanked my lucky star that you are the boy next door. Someday when . . .

Stephanie stopped reading and listened for a moment. "Oh, Allie, you really have to go now? Are you serious? You even have to clean out the closets? Whoa, that's going to take you all the rest of the day. No, don't worry about it. But quick, what do you think? Was it okay so far? Really, Darcy? You aren't just saying that to be nice? Okay, okay. Allie? Huh? Well, of course I'm sending it to him. Well, not sending it exactly. I'll explain later. Good luck with your closets. Bye!"

Stephanie climbed the stairs to her room and

rummaged through her desk drawers. At last she found the box of stationery that Becky had given her for Christmas last year. She'd never even opened the box. Stephanie took off the lid and admired the wild shade of the hot pink paper and the bright black and yellow squiggles in the upper left-hand corner. How had Becky known that someday she, Stephanie Tanner, would need just such a piece of stationery to write the most important letter of her life?

After trying out several different ink colors on the first piece of stationery, Stephanie chose a black felt-tip pen and took out a clean sheet of paper. Then she pulled her letter out of her pocket, unfolded it, and, in her best handwriting, started copying it over.

"What are you doing?" Michelle was standing right beside Stephanie's desk, with Comet at her side.

"What does it look like?" asked Stephanie. "I'm writing a letter."

"Do you have a pen pal? My class might have pen pals later this year."

"Listen, Michelle," said Stephanie, "I can't talk and write at the same time, and I really need to get this letter written."

46

"Okay," said Michelle. "But can you just tell me who you're writing the letter to?"

"Eddie."

"Eddie?" Michelle looked puzzled. "But he lives next door."

"True."

"I thought letters were for people who live far away, like Aunt Gilda."

"Not necessarily."

"But if you have something to say to Eddie, why don't you walk over and say it?"

"Some things are just too important to say face to face. And besides"—Stephanie picked up her piece of stationery and looked at it admiringly—"this way Eddie will have something to keep." She sighed. "Forever."

"Is it a *love* letter?" asked Michelle.

"Not exactly. Now could you please let me . . ."

"I would *never* write a love letter," Michelle declared. "At least not to a yucky boy."

"You might not always feel that way. Oh, no!" Stephanie looked at her paper in horror. "Look what you made me do!"

"What?" said Michelle. "I don't see anything."

Stephanie answered by crumpling her letter

into a ball and tossing it into the wastebasket. "Please, Michelle. I'll talk to you, I promise, just as soon as I finish my letter."

"That's okay," said Michelle. "I think I'll write a love letter too."

"Oh?" said Stephanie. "I thought you said boys are yucky."

"I did," said Michelle. "I'm going to write my love letter to a boy *dog*." She reached down and rumpled the fur on the big dog's head. "Come on, Comet. We have work to do."

Once more, Stephanie focused her attention on copying over her letter. It took only two more false starts before she was satisfied with the results. "There," she said. "Done."

"Me too," said Michelle. "Want to hear mine?" Not waiting for an answer, she began reading:

Dear Comet,
    You are the most best dog in the world and I love you even when you jump up on me with muddy wet paws and you stink sometimes and your breath smells horr tarrb   real bad.
                    Love and woof!
                    Michelle

Michelle glanced sideways at Stephanie. "How do you like it?"

"It's very nice," said Stephanie, still studying her own letter.

Michelle got up and went over to look at her older sister's work of art. "I can't wait till I learn to connect the letters when I write, the way you do." She looked more closely at the letter. "Hey, Steph, you forgot to sign it."

"I didn't forget," Stephanie replied. "Watch." Picking up the bottle of True Love, she sprayed perfume into the air and then waved her letter in the haze. "There," she said, taking a sniff. She folded the letter carefully and slipped it into its hot pink envelope. "Now he'll know who it's from."

"Come on, Comet," said Michelle. "Let's go down to the kitchen and I'll rub your letter with a Milk Bone."

Stephanie followed Michelle out of their room, but instead of going downstairs, she went to D.J.'s room. This time she remembered to knock.

"Come in," called D.J.

Stephanie pushed open the door and saw her sister sitting at her desk, surrounded by her math book and notebook paper filled with awful-looking mathematical equations. D.J. didn't even look up as she entered.

"Are the twins still sleeping?" asked Stephanie.

D.J. eyed the intercom that she'd put on her desk. "I haven't heard a peep so far," she said, "but I know they'll wake up any minute and I'm trying to finish reviewing this chapter before they do, so talk fast. What's doing?"

Stephanie held up the hot pink envelope. "Could you deliver this letter to Eddie at school tomorrow?"

"I guess," said D.J., taking the letter. She held it for a second, then brought it closer to her nose. "Whew! What's in here?"

"Just a letter," said Stephanie. "See, I figure that tomorrow, when all those ninth-grade girls meet Eddie, they'll all be, like, falling in love with him and everything, and he might forget all about me, so I wrote him a letter so he won't. See?"

D.J. slipped the letter into her book bag. "Sure, I'll deliver it for you, Steph, but just tell me one thing. What is that smell?"

"You don't recognize it?" Stephanie walked

to the door, then spun around dramatically to face her sister. "That," she said, "is the scent of True Love."

Back in her own bedroom, True Love still hung in the air. Stephanie threw open a window to let some fresh air into the room. Suddenly, in the yard next door, she saw a sight that nearly made her heart stop. There was the boy next door, standing by a large metal washtub filled with bubbly water. Sitting not too far away, looking on with definite suspicion, was the Saint Bernard next door.

Stephanie turned from the window and flew out the door. Stopping by the bathroom, she grabbed a few necessary items, which she stuffed into a mesh bag. Then she dashed downstairs, calling, "Comet! Here, Comet! Bath time!"

CHAPTER
6

◆ ◀ ◆ ◆

"What a great day for washing a dog!" Stephanie said as she dragged Comet by the collar over to where Eddie stood beside the tub of soapy water.

"Oh, hi, Stephanie," said Eddie. "And hello, Comet."

Comet only had eyes for Max. Wagging his tail frantically, the golden retriever strained against Stephanie's grip to go over and give Max a friendly sniff. But Max just whimpered and slunk over to Eddie. The Saint Bernard appeared to be trying to hide behind his master.

"Aw, Max." Eddie gave his dog's head an affectionate rub. "Comet isn't going to hurt you, boy." Then he looked at Stephanie. "I adopted Max from an animal shelter in L.A.," he said. "One of the workers there told me that when Max was a puppy, he was attacked by a full-grown dog."

"That's awful!" Stephanie exclaimed.

"I know," said Eddie. "Ever since then, he's been scared of other dogs. I tried taking him to a park once, to let him run with the other dogs, but he just stayed glued to my side. So now Max gets his exercise when I take him on long, long walks."

"Isn't Max a Saint Bernard?" asked Stephanie. Eddie nodded.

"I didn't think you could get a purebred dog at an animal shelter."

"Sometimes people get a puppy without realizing how much work it takes to housebreak it and everything," said Eddie. "That's what happened with Max. His owners dropped him off at the shelter one day after he chewed up a pair of shoes."

"That's an awful story," Stephanie said. "Except that it's got a happy ending."

Max peeked out at Comet from behind Eddie's leg. Comet's tail started wagging again.

Ever so slowly, Stephanie let Comet inch toward Max. At first, Max jerked back slightly, but then he stretched in Comet's direction until the two dogs were nose to nose.

"Well, look at that," Eddie whispered. "I think Max has made a friend."

Stephanie let go of Comet's collar, and the two dogs took off across the yard, bounding and leaping and wagging their tails.

Eddie lifted the hose out of the tub and twisted its nozzle to OFF. "Guess the bath can wait," he said, smiling as he watched his dog frolicking with Comet. "Max needs a friend more than he needs a bath, anyway." He turned back to Stephanie. "Do you have time to wait? You can use the tub for Comet when they've worn each other out. If they ever do," he added.

The dogs galloped along the hedge toward Stephanie and Eddie and then tore off again.

"So," said Eddie, "what's D.J. up to today?"

Stephanie shrugged. "Studying for some test or something. But getting back to Max, I think it's great that you saved his life by adopting him."

"Well, I don't think he was in any real danger," said Eddie. "I'm sure someone would have adopted a beautiful puppy like him."

54

Cupping his hands to his mouth, Eddie called, "Max! Come on, boy! Let's get this bath over with!"

"Comet!" Stephanie called. "Come, Comet!"

The two dogs bounded back to their owners, panting hard, their tongues lolling out of their mouths.

"Guests first," said Eddie, extending an arm in the direction of the tub, where a few soap bubbles still floated on top of the water.

"Okay," said Stephanie. "Here goes." She tugged Comet over to the water. "Stay, Comet. Stay." She picked up his front legs, put them into the tub, went around to the dog's rear, pushed a bit, and did the same with his hind legs. "Stay," she cautioned. "Good dog, good Comet."

Stephanie began splashing water on Comet's coat. Eddie handed her a sponge, and then reached in the mesh bag she'd brought. He pulled out two plastic bottles. "This is what you use to wash your *dog*?" he asked, staring in surprise at the Salon Deluxe Shampoo bottle. "And Ultra-Rich Super-Conditioning Treatment for Extra-Silky Hair?"

Stephanie reddened slightly and then

shrugged. "Well, you want your dog to look his best, don't you?"

Stephanie poured some shampoo into one hand, rubbed her hands together, and began massaging the shampoo onto her dog. Comet closed his big brown eyes and submitted to the sudsing.

"Is this what D.J. uses on her hair?" asked Eddie.

"What?" said Stephanie, lathering Comet all over.

"This Deluxe stuff," said Eddie. "Is this what makes her hair all shiny like that?"

"Actually, this is what makes my uncle Jesse's hair all shiny," said Stephanie as she coaxed Comet out of the tub. "And he'd kill me if he ever found out I used his precious hair stuff on a dog." Slowly turning the hose nozzle until the water pressure was a gentle stream, she began rinsing Comet, from his head down to his paws.

Meanwhile, Eddie coaxed Max into the tub and gave him his bath. When both dogs were rinsed, Stephanie applied Ultra-Rich Super-Conditioning Treatment for Extra-Silky Hair to each one's coat, let it sit for the required three minutes, and then rinsed it off.

56

Eddie jogged over to his garage and brought back two old beach towels. "Sorry, doggies, no blow-dry service today," he joked, handing Stephanie a towel. She dried Comet while Eddie dried Max.

After Eddie emptied the water into the drain in the driveway, he said, "Well, I'd better take Max inside before he gets all dirty all over again." He picked up the shampoo and rinse from the grass, put them back into the mesh bag, and handed it to Stephanie.

"Thanks," said Stephanie. Then, trying to stop the most wonderful afternoon of her life from being over, she added, "If you and Max ever want any company on your long, long walks, you can count us in."

Eddie looked happy to hear this. "Great! You want to go tomorrow?"

"Tomorrow?" said Stephanie. "But tomorrow's Monday, a school day."

"Before school," said Eddie. "Meet me out front, say around six?"

"Six?" Stephanie's voice squeaked with disbelief. "In the *morning*?"

"Yeah," said Eddie. "But, listen, if that's too early for you . . ."

"No!" said Stephanie. "Too early?" She made herself laugh. "No, no, I was just afraid that might be too *late* to go and, you know, get back in time to get ready for school."

"You're right," said Eddie. "I'll meet you out front at quarter to six. That way we'll have an hour to walk and plenty of time to get ready for . . . school." Eddie barely got the last word out.

Stephanie understood. "Guess you're not exactly looking forward to starting a new school, huh?"

"Not exactly." Eddie shrugged.

Stephanie smiled, secretly pleased that her letter would be there, waiting for him, helping him make it through his first day.

"But what choice do I have?" Eddie continued. "Anyway, I'll see you and Comet tomorrow morning."

"By the way," said Stephanie, "do you take Max for an early walk every single morning?"

"More like every other morning or so," said Eddie. "See you at five forty-five."

Oh, please, thought Stephanie. *Say quarter to six. It sounds so much later.*

*　　*　　*

The second Stephanie and Comet walked in through the kitchen door, Vicki ran over to greet them. "Stephanie!" she said, giving her a big hug. "How's my favorite sixth grader?"

Stephanie hugged Vicki back.

"Hi, Steph," said Steve, who was holding both Alex and Nicky.

"Hi," Stephanie said. "Where's D.J.?"

"Still hitting the books," Steve replied. "She'll be down for dinner."

"How was your afternoon, honey?" her father asked. "Did you get that writing finished?"

"All done," said Stephanie happily. "I came up with a perfect idea. And speaking of perfect, take a look at Comet."

"Comet!" called Danny. "Here, boy!"

Comet galloped over, and Danny patted the big dog. "My, my, you're a clean boy now, yes, you are," crooned Danny. He stood up, nodding. "Nice work, Stephanie."

Michelle came over and gave Comet a big hug. "Yum, now I can write you a love letter about how good you smell," she said.

"My turn," said Jesse. He too petted Comet and then exclaimed, "Comet, baby, your coat is fabulous!" He ran his hands along Comet's back and gave Stephanie a suspicious glance. "You know, the only other time I felt hair this soft and manageable and *silky*, it was *my* hair."

Stephanie gave Jesse one of the biggest smiles she could manage while repositioning the mesh bag behind her back.

"Well, Comet," said Becky, "I hope you know Jesse has just given you the ultimate compliment."

Jesse's eyes never left Stephanie. "Do you know that this morning all I could find to wash my hair with was someone else's dandruff shampoo?" Jesse shuddered. "You wouldn't know what happened to my bottle of Ultra-Rich Super-Conditioning Treatment for Extra-Silky Hair, would you, Steph? My *fifteen-dollar* bottle?"

"Uh . . . Gee, Uncle Jesse, I think I saw it somewhere recently. Very recently."

Jesse leaned over to see what might be inside the bag.

Sheepishly, Stephanie brought it out from behind her back. "Sorry, Uncle Jesse," she said. "It was sort of . . . sort of a dog-washing emergency. I'll pay for the amount I used."

"That won't be necessary." Jesse sniffed. "I just hope you rinsed Comet thoroughly."

"Absolutely," said Stephanie. "I owe you a favor, Uncle Jesse," she added. "A big one."

"Deal." Jesse took the shampoo and cream rinse and hugged them to his chest. "I'm just glad to have my good stuff back."

Comet jumped up, put his paws on Jesse's chest, and licked his face.

"Whoa!" said Jesse, laughing. "Okay, okay, boy. My hair products are your hair products. I'm very happy to have a dog who appreciates the finer things in life. That's right. We don't want to wash our hair with any old dandruff shampoo, do we?"

"Speaking of *itch*, kids," said Joey as D.J. came down the stairs, "let me fill you in on *The Big Itch*."

"I heard it was really scary and suspenseful," said D.J.

"Yeah, see, these giant ants invade Los Angeles," Joey explained. "They take over all the beaches, they take over Disneyland. Then, on the night of the Academy Awards . . . But, hey, you might want to see it, and I don't want to ruin the ending for you."

"I don't think so," said Stephanie. "Anyway,

I can't believe you all went to see a movie about giant bugs."

"It was the only movie at the Multiplex that none of us had seen," said Jesse. "And no one but me was willing to go down to the Coronet to see Elvis in *Viva Las Vegas!*" He shrugged. "So the creepy crawlers won out."

Dinner that night was pizza. After eating two slices, Stephanie asked to be excused. "Got to get ready for bed," she said.

"At eight fifteen?" asked her father.

"Well, I've been worrying that Comet isn't getting enough exercise," Stephanie explained, "so I'm taking him for an early morning walk."

"Good night, Steph," said Becky. "And I'm happy that you found a writing topic you really care about."

"Me too," Stephanie said, giving D.J. a quick look. "Me too."

CHAPTER
7

Stephanie glanced at her watch as she and Comet staggered up their front steps. Six forty-five. The brisk morning walk with the boy next door and the dog next door had taken exactly one hour. But Stephanie thought that *walk* wasn't exactly the right word for what they had been doing. *Run* would be a better word. The words *race* and *sprint* and *marathon* also came to mind.

At the top of the steps Comet flopped down on his side, breathing heavily. Stephanie sat down beside the panting dog to catch her own breath. Eddie could at least have mentioned yesterday that he used to be on the track team at his old school, and that his event was the two-mile run. But of course, Stephanie thought, that might have been bragging, and Eddie would never do such a thing.

Gathering her strength, Stephanie got to her feet and opened the front door. Both she and the dog headed for the kitchen, where Stephanie opened the refrigerator and poured herself a tall glass of orange juice while Comet beelined for his water bowl. After the juice, Stephanie gulped down two big bowls of cereal and then went upstairs to take a shower.

Weekday mornings in the Tanner household could be confusing, with seven people wanting to take seven showers in three bathrooms all within an hour. The house rule was: A THREE-MINUTE SHOWER. That way, everyone got a turn and there was hot water for all. It only got confusing when someone lost track of the time. Unfortunately this seemed to be one of those mornings.

When Stephanie went into the bathroom, Michelle was at the sink brushing her teeth and D.J. was already in the shower. "D.J.!" Stephanie called. "Hurry up!"

"Okay, okay!" said D.J. At last she stepped

out of the shower stall and wrapped a towel around herself. Looking right at Stephanie but appearing not to notice her, she muttered, "The range of the data is the difference between the greatest and the least numbers."

"I knew that," Stephanie said. After her shower she whipped on her favorite blue-jean skirt and a white shirt with rhinestones on the pockets. She hurtled down the stairs in time to catch D.J. walking out the door.

"Hold it!" Stephanie called. She caught up with her sister going down the front steps. "Okay, D.J., don't forget."

"I won't forget," said D.J. as they reached the street and turned toward the bus stop, "that the most common numeral in a series is the mode."

"The *letter*," said Stephanie. "Don't forget to give Eddie my letter! Okay?"

For a second D.J. looked blankly at Stephanie, and then her eyes showed a spark of understanding. "The True Love letter," she said, and patted her book bag. "Got it right here."

"*Please* remember every single thing he says when he reads it, okay? Okay, D.J.?" Stephanie pleaded.

D.J. nodded.

"What time are you getting home this afternoon?" asked Stephanie.

"If I survive this test," said D.J., "I'll be home right after school."

Just then Steve pulled alongside the curb in his sports car.

D.J. smiled and waved. "And if Steve gives me a ride home from school, I'll beat you home."

"Hi, D.J.! Hi, Steph!" called Steve. "Come on, D.J. I'll give you a lift to school."

D.J. headed over to the car. "See you tonight, Steph," she said. "And don't worry about your you-know-what."

Stephanie smiled as she waved to her sister, and then walked on alone toward the bus stop. Steve was a nice guy, she reflected. And he'd be even nicer if he didn't have a two-seater car. She wouldn't mind getting a lift to school once in a while. Oh, well. She could see Allie and Darcy up at the corner. She sure had a lot to fill them in on while they waited for the bus.

"Really?" asked Darcy. She was wearing black jeans and a new burgundy crushed-velvet shirt that looked great against her dark skin. A silver hand charm on a black silk cord dangled from her neck. "You really asked D.J. to give Eddie your letter?"

Stephanie nodded. "I told you I was going to, didn't I? And I'm really glad, too, because Eddie was dreading starting a new school and all, and my letter will cheer him up for sure."

"That is so cool," said Allie, who had on a top just like Darcy's, only in navy, a wide brown leather belt, and a pair of loose-fitting jeans. "You, Stephanie Tanner, age eleven, have a high school boyfriend."

For a second, panic gripped Stephanie. She didn't really like the sound of that. Of course, she *was* eleven. And Eddie *was* in the first year of high school. But Allie's description made it sound as if there were really lots and lots of difference in their ages when, in fact, Eddie was barely fourteen. Three measly years. No big deal.

On the bus, Allie and Darcy took two seats together while Stephanie took the one across the aisle. She told her friends all about the romantic dog-washing episode with Eddie and about their early morning run.

"You think you'll do that every morning?" asked Darcy.

"I don't know," said Stephanie, a wave of exhaustion washing over her. "I want to, like, be with him, but all that running might do me in."

Stephanie's first class on Monday was English, her favorite, taught by Mrs. Burns, her favorite teacher. But today as Mrs. Burns called on students to give her a list of lively verbs to write on the board, Stephanie let her mind wander over to the high school. By this time, she imagined, D.J. had found Eddie and given him her letter. She pictured him taking it, holding it to his nose and breathing in deeply, but not opening it. Not right away. He'd probably go off somewhere by himself, to some deserted part of the hallway. Then he'd open the envelope and take out her letter. . . . But just as he was about to read it, a girl would come over to him. . . .

"Hi, there," a tall, beautiful ninth-grade girl is saying to the new boy. "You're new here, aren't you? What's your name?"

"Eddie," says Eddie, never looking up from the letter he is reading.

"Boy, that letter you're reading must be

really good," says the blond girl, " 'cause you haven't even taken your eyes off it to look at me, and I'm the most gorgeous girl in the whole ninth grade. Do you want to be my new boyfriend?"

Now Eddie looks at her, but only shakes his head. "Sorry," he says, "I'm already going out with Stephanie. Stephanie Tanner."

"Stephanie Tanner?" says the girl rather loudly. "Stephanie Tanner? Stephanie Tanner!"

"Stephanie Tanner!"
Stephanie blinked and looked up into the face of Mrs. Burns, who was standing right beside her desk. For a moment, Stephanie had no sense at all of where she was. "Excuse me, Mrs. Burns," she managed. "What did you say?"

"I asked for a rough draft of your story for the Golden Gate Creative Writing Contest, Stephanie," said Mrs. Burns, an impatient tone in her voice. "May I have it, please?"

"I . . . uh, I wrote one over the weekend, Mrs. Burns," Stephanie began, "but it wasn't quite right. Could I have until the end of the day to give it to you?"

The teacher sighed. "Until the end of lunch period, Stephanie. And if I don't get it, I'm taking a whole letter off this term's grade. That's only fair."

Stephanie nodded.

"As always," continued Mrs. Burns, "I'm expecting something wonderful from you."

Stephanie's heart sank as she thought of how she'd have to write during math class and fake a twisted ankle so she could work during gym. Then she had a study hall. Great! Then lunch. For sure she could work through lunch. Well, maybe she could get Mrs. Burns something by the end of lunch period. But something *wonderful*? She wasn't so sure.

"Genius at work," said Darcy, holding up a hand to stop one of their friends who approached the long cafeteria table where Stephanie sat writing at breakneck speed. "She can't talk now."

"Ready for another bite?" asked Allie.

In answer, Stephanie opened her mouth, and Allie stuck in a forkful of mashed potatoes.

Just as the bell rang to end the third lunch period, Stephanie slammed down her pencil and shouted, "Done!"

"Yeah!" yelled Allie and Darcy together.

"Well, Mrs. Burns said 'rough draft,' and this one brings new meaning to the word *rough*, but at least it's finished." Stephanie let out a big breath as she gathered her papers. "I owe you guys big time," she said. "I never would have finished it if you hadn't helped. Thanks a lot."

"So what's it about?" asked Allie.

"It's called 'No Big Deal,' " said Stephanie as the three friends got up from the cafeteria table and carried their trays over to the conveyor belt. "You know how Mrs. Burns always says to write about what you know?"

Allie and Darcy nodded.

"So I did. It's about a girl who has a big crush on a boy who's three years older than she is," explained Stephanie. "The story is sort of like my letter to Eddie. You know—all about how this girl really likes and admires this older boy. Only in the story I could go all out about my . . . er, the girl's feelings, because Eddie will never read my story. If he ever did, he'd know it was about him, except that I made it take place in the twenty-first century."

"You mean," said Darcy, "that it's a futuristic story of doomed love?"

"Not at all!" said Stephanie brightly. "See, the boy really, really likes the girl too. A lot. At first he does think that she's too young for him. But by the twenty-first century, people have really long life spans, and when he's one hundred and twenty-five years old, she'll be one hundred and twenty-two years old, so he realizes that their age difference turns out to be *no big deal*, and they live happily ever after."

"Oh," breathed Allie, "that is so romantic."

"It is," agreed Darcy. "A story of true love."

CHAPTER
8

That afternoon on the bus home, Stephanie didn't say much to Darcy and Allie. She was tired from getting up so early, and her muscles were starting to ache from all the running. Her mind was worn out by all her frantic work on her story for the Golden Gate Creative Writing Contest, so she contented herself with listening to Darcy and Allie describe the clothes they were setting aside for the big three-way clothes swap, which was to take place in two weeks. Half listening, that is, because Stephanie could hardly keep her thoughts away from running upstairs to D.J.'s room the second she got home and hearing every detail of Eddie getting her letter.

Once she walked through her front door, however, Stephanie found other things to think about.

Uncle Jesse was sitting on the couch, entertaining Alex and Nicky. "Boy, am I glad to see you!" he said.

"Uh-oh," Stephanie replied. "Hey, is D.J. home yet?"

"She's upstairs," said Jesse. "Listen, Steph, Joey just called and we may have a gig this weekend, but I've got to deliver a demo tape. It'll only take a little while, so . . . think you could handle Nicky and Alex until I get home?"

"Sure, sure, anything," said Stephanie, heading for the stairs. "Just give me fifteen minutes upstairs with D.J. and I'll take care of the twins for the rest of their lives."

"I don't have *two* minutes to spare," said Jesse. "If I don't get there right away, the deal will fall through. And we could use this one, Steph."

Stephanie stopped in her tracks.

"Plus," said Jesse, "I think you were the girl

who said she owed me a favor?" Jesse hummed a few bars from the advertising ditty for Ultra-Rich Super-Conditioning Treatment for Extra-Silky Hair.

"Gotcha," said Stephanie, coming back into the living room and taking Nicky and Alex by their sticky little hands. "Come on, guys. Wave bye-bye to Daddy!"

"Bye!" called Jesse as he hurtled out the door. "And thanks, Steph. Thanks a million!"

"So," said Stephanie once she was alone with the twins, "you two look like you want to practice climbing stairs this afternoon, am I right?"

"No!" Alex shouted. "No 'tairs."

"But if we climb up the stairs, we can go visit D.J. Wouldn't you like to see D.J. up in her room?"

"No!" Nicky chimed in. "No Dee."

"This is so frustrating!" said Stephanie. "D.J. is two floors above my head and I am desperate to talk to her, but I can't get up there. Isn't that frustrating?"

"No!" the boys shouted together. "No! No! NO!"

With a sudden flash of inspiration, Stephanie

picked up the phone and dialed D.J.'s best friend.

"Kimmy? Is that you?"

"I am I," Kimmy replied. "Is that you, squirt?"

"Listen, Kimmy, I'm stuck down on the ground floor watching the twins and . . ."

"Those rug rats are dangerous!" Kimmy warned. "Don't let them out of your sight! When I sat for them last week, I turned my head for one second, and in no time they had finger-painted the entire dining room wall green."

"Kimmy, you finally confessed that you had watched a whole episode of *90210* while the boys were by themselves."

"Yeah, well, it felt like about a second. So, what can I do for you, Tanner?"

"Would you call our number and ask D.J. to come downstairs right away because I really, *really* need to talk to her? Hang on. Nicky! Let go of Comet's tail. I mean it, Nicky. Kimmy? I have to go. Call D.J., okay?"

"You got it."

As Stephanie ran to rescue the dog, she heard the phone ring. After only two rings it stopped.

Stephanie was sure D.J. had picked up and would be down in a flash. But one minute turned into two and there was no sign of her. Impatiently, Stephanie picked up the phone, only to hear Kimmy and D.J. talking about their last prom committee meeting.

"Hey!" Stephanie cried into the receiver. "Kimmy! Didn't you give D.J. my message?"

"Oops!" said Kimmy. "Must have slipped my mind. D.J., your sister wants you to come downstairs right away."

"Thanks so much, Kimmy," Stephanie said sarcastically. "D.J., can you please come down? *Please?* I want to hear all about Eddie getting my letter, and I can't come up because I'm watching the . . . Alex! No! Yucky! No, no! Don't put that CD in your mouth! D.J., please?"

"I'll be right down," said D.J., "but to tell you the truth, Steph, there isn't that much to tell."

"What!" Stephanie cried. "Didn't you deliver it?"

"I did," said D.J., "but not in person. Listen, by the time I went to the office and chatted up the secretary to find out where Eddie's locker was . . ."

"Hold it a sec," said Stephanie. "You can hang up now, Kimmy."

"Now? Not a chance. Go on, D.J."

"Anyway, I waited at his locker until about two seconds before my stat test was about to start and I really couldn't wait any longer, so I just stuck the letter into his locker and ran to my class."

"Are you *sure* you got the right locker?" Stephanie asked.

"Positive," said D.J.

"Nicky!" Stephanie cried. "That's Comet's dish. Now put it down."

"I'll come down and help," said D.J., and she hung up.

Just as Stephanie pried the dog's dish out of her little cousin's hand, the doorbell rang.

"Coming!" Stephanie called as she carried Alex and Nicky to the couch.

Stephanie ran to the door, calling out, "Who is it?"

"Eddie!" came a voice from the other side of the door.

Stephanie gasped. Hoping that she looked

okay, she opened the door and said, "Hi, Eddie! Come on in!"

"Oh, is it dinnertime?" Eddie asked, looking at the dog dish in Stephanie's hand.

Stephanie's face reddened. "I just wrestled it away from Nicky when the doorbell rang." She eyed the little boys, who had actually stayed on the couch. "So, how was, you know, everything at school, Eddie?"

"Not too bad," Eddie said as he stepped across the threshold. "The kids seem pretty nice, none of my teachers bit my head off or anything, and . . ." Eddie smiled almost slyly as he added, "I found a very nice surprise inside my locker."

Eddie looked really happy, Stephanie thought. Happier than she'd ever seen him. And then she saw, peeking out of Eddie's jacket pocket, just a sliver of a hot pink envelope. "So, you were sort of surprised?"

"Not *sort of* surprised. Really surprised." Now Eddie's face was starting to get a little red. "I mean, I hoped that, well, that the girl next door would think about me the way I thought about her, but I just never thought it would be quite—" he shrugged—"quite this good."

Stephanie heard footsteps on the stairs. Oh, no! Why did someone have to show up now, right at the most romantic moment of her whole life?

"Hey, Eddie," said D.J., walking into the living room. "So, how did your first day go?"

"Great," said Eddie, "thanks to you, D.J."

"Me?" Puzzled at first, D.J. then broke into a smile. "Oh, you mean the letter . . ."

"Yeah," said Eddie. "I mean the letter. It was really, really incredible."

"Yeah?" said D.J. "That's great. Listen, Steph, you two probably have things to talk about, so why don't I take over on twin duty?"

"Thanks, D.J.," said Stephanie, making a mental note to get D.J. something really incredibly wonderful for her next birthday.

"Let's go, boys," D.J. began.

"But, D.J.," said Eddie, looking confused, "don't you think you and I should be the ones to talk? I mean, all that stuff you said in your letter . . ."

"No," said D.J., frowning. "There's a mix-up here. That letter's not from me, Eddie. It's . . . it's . . ."

"It's what, D.J.?" said Eddie. "It's a big secret or something? Okay, I can keep a secret, but don't deny that it's your letter. I happened to be just down the hall this morning before school, and I saw you put this"—he pulled the hot pink envelope from his jacket pocket—"in my locker."

Stephanie could hardly believe her ears. Or her eyes. Didn't Eddie have any kind of nose at all? Didn't he realize that she wore True Love and not D.J.? Didn't he understand that she and only she could have written the words, those carefully chosen words, that had been inside that hot pink envelope?

"But I only . . ." D.J. began. "Uh, that is—"

"What D.J. means," Stephanie cut in quickly, "is that she wrote you that letter so you wouldn't feel really alone on your first day of school. But that was all. It was really . . . no big deal."

It hadn't been easy for Stephanie to get those words out. Now that she had, she could feel her heart pounding like crazy.

Eddie looked confused and hurt. "Is that true, D.J.? Is it?"

But before D.J. had a chance to answer, the front door opened again and Jesse and Joey burst in.

"Well, we got the job!" Jesse bounced over to Stephanie and gave her a high five. Then he picked up the twins and twirled them around, chanting, "We got the job! We got the job!"

"Yes!" said Joey. "Hey, listen, guys. Want to hear a good one I heard at the studio this afternoon?" And without waiting for an answer, he started in. "See, there was this man who took his dog, Fido, to the movie, and at every really funny part throughout the whole movie, Fido laughed and laughed. After the picture was over, the woman who'd been sitting behind Fido tapped the dog's owner on the shoulder and said, 'Excuse me, sir, but I'm really amazed at your dog. Why, he actually seemed to enjoy this film!' And Fido's owner said, 'Believe me, ma'am, I'm just as surprised as you are by Fido's reaction, because, you know, he simply hated the book.' "

D.J. and Eddie laughed politely. Stephanie could barely manage a smile. After an awkward pause, D.J said, "Well, I've got homework."

And with that, she turned and went up the stairs.

"Me too," said Eddie. He let himself out the front door.

With tears welling up in her eyes, Stephanie raced up the stairs. If only D.J. would keep her secret! Then Eddie wouldn't think that she was a total jerk.

"D.J.?" Stephanie knocked on her sister's door.

D.J. opened the door and gave Stephanie a big hug. "What a mess, huh?" she said.

"I can't believe Eddie has a major crush on you." Stephanie moaned as both girls walked over to D.J.'s bed and sat down. "The love of my life is in love with my own sister. Isn't that against the law or something?"

"It should be," said D.J.

"Oh, why didn't I just keep writing about our troubled planet?" Stephanie said. "Then none of this would have happened. But anyway, thanks for not telling Eddie who really wrote the letter. And is it okay? What I said? I mean, how I said that the letter really was from you?"

"Don't worry about it, Steph. I can handle it.

But since I'm supposed to be the author of this letter, how about telling me what it says."

"Nothing mushy, if that's what you're worried about," Stephanie said. "I told him that I never dreamed someone like him would move in next door. And that until I met him, everyone just thought I was just a kid, but that he helped me to show, well, you know, my serious side."

"Is that true?" D.J. asked. "Do you really feel that Eddie brings out a serious side of you?"

Stephanie nodded. "I guess around here I'm always joking around and trying to make people laugh, and if sometimes I feel like being serious, people say, 'Oh, Stephanie, that doesn't sound like you.' " Stephanie flopped down on the bed and stared up at the ceiling. "Have you ever gotten things this snarled up?" she asked. "I mean with a boy?"

D.J. looked thoughtful. "Well, there was Ned Cardone."

"Who's he?"

"He was in seventh grade when I was in sixth," said D.J., "and I was madly in love with him. At least I thought I was for a couple of weeks. At that time, some boys were buying girls these silver chains with little round medallions with their initials on them. Anyway, I was too shy to even talk to Ned, so I went over to the mall, all by myself, and I bought one of those medallions and had Ned's initials engraved on it: N.C."

Stephanie giggled. "And you wore it to school?"

"Of course! That was the whole point—to show Ned that I liked him."

"So? Did he get the message?"

"He got it, all right," said D.J. "The only trouble was, Ned had a big crush on Kimmy."

"Bad idea!" Stephanie exclaimed.

"And," D.J. continued, "over the same weekend, Ned had gone to the mall and bought his own medallion and had it engraved with N.C. and had given it to Kimmy. So there we were, on Monday morning, with these twin N.C. medallions on."

"What happened?"

D.J. shook her head. "Well, Kimmy was furious. She thought that Ned had actually bought me my medallion too, even though at first I told her it was from some boy she didn't know named Nigel Combs."

"Nigel Combs!" Stephanie couldn't help but burst out laughing.

"I know it's weird, but I didn't have much time to think about it. Then I said the initials stood for the state of North Carolina. Finally, when I told her the truth, she didn't believe me. So at lunch period, she gave Ned his medallion back and then punched him in the stomach."

"Poor Ned Cardone," Stephanie said.

"You're right," said D.J. "And it was all my fault."

"Well, not entirely," said Stephanie. "Kimmy's an animal."

D.J. laughed. Then she got up from her bed and walked over to her dresser. Opening her jewelry box, she dug around for a minute and then lifted out a very tarnished and tangled silver chain from which hung a nearly black disk. "This is it," she said, walking back over to her sister.

Stephanie could barely make out the initials N.C. on the disk. "I'm surprised you still have it."

"I've kept it all these years," said D.J., "as a kind of reminder that not being totally honest can lead to a very tangled up situation." D.J. held up the knotted chain. "And now you've got your own tangle to worry about."

Stephanie frowned. "True. Letting Eddie think that you wrote the letter isn't honest, is it?"

"Listen, Steph," said D.J., "I won't tell Eddie about the letter. I promise. But one of these days, maybe you should."

Stephanie sighed. "You're right. And I will. Even if it means he'll think I'm a dope *and* a liar."

"He won't think like that, Steph. Really. He'll be flattered that you cared enough to write the letter in the first place. And he'll understand that since he was the one who was mixed up about who wrote it, you'd be embarrassed to say you did."

"I guess," said Stephanie.

"Besides," said D.J., "Eddie's going to have a million other things to think about—being in a new school, new kids, new homework, a new school paper to write for, a new track team. He's not going to give this thing too much thought."

Stephanie got up from D.J.'s bed and gave

her sister a hug. "I feel slightly less tangled up now," she said.

D.J. smiled. "Really?"

"Really," said Stephanie. "I'll just go next door and tell Eddie the truth about the letter and this whole mess will be over."

"That's the spirit," said D.J. "Go on and get it over with."

But Stephanie didn't move.

"Well," said D.J., "are you going over to Eddie's?"

"Yep, I'm going over there," Stephanie said firmly, "first thing tomorrow."

CHAPTER

9

◆ ◀ ◆ ◆

Stephanie didn't have a chance to tell Allie and Darcy about the letter fiasco until the next day at lunch. Allie was horrified by the story.

"If that had happened to me, I'd beg my parents to send me to boarding school so I wouldn't have to face Eddie ever again," she said with a shudder.

"You would?" said Stephanie, getting worried all over again.

"It's not that serious, Allie," Darcy said. "Besides, Eddie doesn't even know you wrote the letter, Steph, so what's the big deal?"

"I have to tell him," said Stephanie. "Not today or anything. But sometime."

"Why?" Allie asked. "Why not leave things just the way they are?"

"Because it's not fair for Eddie to think that D.J. would write a letter like that and then consider it no big deal. And it's not fair to D.J., either."

"I see your point," said Darcy. "But, hey, in the meantime, how about getting yourself a sixth-grade boyfriend?"

"Yeah," said Allie. "There goes Jon Sacher, over by the conveyor belt. He's cute, and he doesn't like Liliana anymore."

"Not my type," said Stephanie.

"What about Andrew Zebell?" Darcy asked. "If I didn't like Evan Cotton, I'd like Andrew myself."

"No, he's not my type, either," said Stephanie.

"Picky, picky," Allie scolded. "So, who is your type?"

"His initials are E.S.," said Stephanie. "Eddie Schwab."

"Boy," said Allie, picking up her tray as lunch hour ended, "this must be love."

The three girls walked to English class together and took their seats. Mrs. Burns returned everyone's story for the Golden Gate Creative Writing Contest with her comments and gave the class the entire period to work on their revisions.

At first glance, Stephanie saw only lots of red ink on her story, and her heart sank. Of course she should have proofread the story, but there hadn't been time! But as she settled down and began reading the comments, she felt better. Aside from quite a few spelling errors on the first page, she also read: "Nice description, Stephanie!" and "This conversation really lets me know how the two characters are feeling." And on the last page, Mrs. Burns had written: "This is a very funny story with well-developed characters and a nice surprise at the end. I'd like to see you describe the setting a bit more."

Stephanie got out a sharp pencil and went to work on her story. If she couldn't have Eddie Schwab's love and devotion, she could at least express her feelings of love through her characters. Instead of devoting herself to Eddie, she would devote herself to becoming a fabulously rich and famous writer—that's what she'd do. Stephanie smiled as she began adding details to the setting and beefing up her characters' dialogue. She was so involved in her story that she never even heard the end-of-the-period bell ringing.

"You may go now, Stephanie," said Mrs. Burns.

Stephanie looked up from her paper and saw that the classroom was empty. She was the only one still sitting there. Mrs. Burns sat at her desk, smiling at Stephanie.

That night after dinner, Stephanie perched at the kitchen counter and continued her revision.

"How's it going, honey?" her father asked.

"Great," said Stephanie, finishing the sentence she was working on and then looking up. "Of course it doesn't have a chance in the contest, but I like it."

"Why doesn't it have a chance?" Becky asked. "I'm sure you're as good a writer as any sixth grader in San Francisco."

"It's not that," said Stephanie. "It's just that my story's sort of on the funny side, and the judges in these contests only pick stories with really serious themes."

"Such as 'Interview with a Dying Planet'?" Joey suggested.

"Exactly," said Stephanie. "But I don't care about winning. At least my story will give Mrs. Burns and the judges a few chuckles."

"If they have to read many compositions like 'Interview with a Dying Planet,'" said Joey, "they'll be incredibly grateful to you, Steph."

"Thanks, Joey. Hey, there's the phone. I bet it's Allie. I'll get it!" Stephanie ran into the living room, picked up the phone, and said, "Hello?"

"Hi, Steph. It's Eddie."

"Eddie!" The word came out like a croak.

"Steph? Are you okay?"

"Uh, yeah, yeah," Stephanie said, trying to sound casual.

"Okay, well, listen, I was just wondering if you wanted to walk Comet with Max and me again tomorrow morning."

Stephanie gulped. She wasn't ready to face Eddie and tell him the truth. Thinking quickly, she said, "Oh, well, thanks anyway, Eddie. But I was pretty wiped out by yesterday morning's walk—which was really what I'd call more of a run—but anyway, I don't think so."

"Oh," said Eddie. "Okay, well, bye."

"Bye."

Slowly, Stephanie hung up the phone. Looking down, she saw Comet sitting beside her, thumping his tail and looking very cheerful. "I just saved you from another six-mile run," she told the dog, and she thought she could almost hear him sigh with relief.

Michelle walked into the living room just then, and the phone rang again.

"Michelle, answer it, will you? And if it's Eddie, I'm not home!"

"You want me to tell a big lie for you?" Michelle asked.

"Yes!" Stephanie shouted. "I mean, no! Just say I can't come to the phone, okay? That's not a lie. I can't talk to him, really."

"Hello?" said Michelle. "Hold on. I'll see if she can come to the phone." Then in a loud whisper she said, "It's Allie. Can you come to the phone?"

Stephanie snatched the phone away from her little sister and settled into the couch. "Allie, am I glad to hear from you. You won't believe what just happened. Okay, sure, I'll hold. That way I can tell you and Darcy at the same time."

After the girls had discussed Eddie's phone call for twenty minutes, Darcy announced that she had to hang up. "But, Steph, are you okay about Eddie?" she asked.

"I guess," said Stephanie. "As long as I don't have to see him or talk to him until I'm one hundred percent over him, I'll be okay."

"How long do you think that'll take?" asked Allie.

"I don't know," said Stephanie. "Probably about fifty years."

CHAPTER
10

♦ ◄ ♦ ♦

On Wednesday, at the end of English class, Stephanie handed in her revision of "No Big Deal" to Mrs. Burns.

The teacher took the story and smiled. "You know, your first draft showed real promise, Stephanie," she said.

"Thanks, Mrs. Burns. I'll keep my fingers crossed that the judges will like it."

But in truth, Stephanie didn't give her story another thought for the rest of the week. She had something far more important to occupy her mind, and that was avoiding Eddie Schwab. Luckily, Michelle was willing—for twenty-five cents a morning—to watch out the window and tell her when Eddie left for school. That way, Stephanie could leave when the coast was clear. Coming home from school might have been trickier, except that D.J. told Stephanie that Eddie had joined the track team, which practiced after school.

Saturday, Stephanie and Allie went over to Darcy's house. They tuned in to *Teen Scene* to check out what Bay Area kids were on this popular local show and what they were wearing, and then gave each other facials. Allie had to go home before dinner, but Stephanie spent the night. On Sunday it was drizzling. Darcy and Allie came over to the Tanners' and the three girls watched videos.

For seven days, one entire week, Stephanie successfully avoided seeing Eddie Schwab. And since she hadn't seen him, she actually managed not to think about him all that much.

The only thing that kept Stephanie from being 100 percent contented with her life was that she hadn't yet told Eddie the truth about the letter. Well, she would. One of these days. When she was ready. Soon. Very soon.

The following Wednesday afternoon, as Stephanie sat down at her desk in English class, she noticed Mrs. Burns smiling at her strangely. *What did I do now?* Stephanie wondered. She couldn't think of a thing, but when Mrs. Burns called the class to order, her mind was still turning over possible problems. And so it came as a total shock when Mrs. Burns said, "Class, I am so very pleased and proud to announce that someone from this class has won the sixth-grade first place in the Golden Gate Creative Writing Contest. Our winner is Stephanie Tanner!"

Stephanie felt her smile stretching practically from ear to ear. The judges picked a funny story as the winner after all. Well, this was it! The first step toward her dream of becoming a really rich and famous writer. She could almost see her name—Stephanie Tanner—in lovely, curvy script letters on the jacket of a big fat book.

"Is there a prize for this contest?" Liliana asked. "Or is it just one of those honor things?"

"Well, there's no money award, Liliana, if that's what you mean, but it's a great honor," Mrs. Burns said. "And it's one that the whole city will know about, because all the winning stories are going to be published in the *San Francisco Dispatch* this coming Friday."

Wow! thought Stephanie. *My very own story, in the newspaper for everybody to read. My story in the newspaper for Eddie Schwab to read and figure out that . . .*

"Wait!" Stephanie sprang out of her chair. "What if the contest winners don't *want* their story published in the newspaper?"

"Oh, Stephanie," said Mrs. Burns, "there's no need to be modest. Now, everyone please get out your *Language for Daily Use* and open it to chapter seven."

After class, Stephanie tried again. "Mrs. Burns, I really don't want my story printed in the paper. It has nothing to do with being modest. It has to do with . . . something else."

The English teacher put her arm around Stephanie's shoulders. "Don't you know that your winning the contest brings honor on all of us here at John Muir Middle School? You wouldn't want to deprive us of this honor, would you?"

"Well, no . . ." Stephanie began. "But do you think the paper could just give my name? And your name, as my English teacher, without printing the story?"

Mrs. Burns laughed. "I'm afraid not, Stephanie. Anyway, it's too late. The winning stories have probably already been printed."

Stephanie sighed. "Okay, Mrs. Burns," she said. "Thanks anyway."

On the way home on the bus, Stephanie talked her problem over with Allie and Darcy. "If Eddie reads two paragraphs of my story, he'll know it's about me having a major crush on him."

"But maybe he won't read it," said Darcy. "I hardly ever read the paper myself."

"But he will!" Stephanie protested. "He's a big paper reader, and he's very interested in newspaper writing because he wants to be a journalist! He'll read the story and he'll know how I had such a crush on him. Plus he'll know right away that D.J. never wrote the letter to him and that I did. I really meant to tell him the truth, only I haven't gotten around to it, and, oh, my life is over!"

"Maybe the paper hasn't printed the stories yet," said Allie. "You know how they always wait until the last minute to see if anything more important comes along."

Stephanie brightened slightly. "Yeah, maybe," she said. "Listen, can you both come over today for a little while? You'd really be a help to me in gathering up my courage."

"Courage?' said Darcy. "For what?"

"For calling the *Dispatch*," said Stephanie.

At the Tanners' house, the three girls wrote down a little speech that they felt was just right for talking with someone from the newspaper. Then Darcy found the main number for the *Dispatch* in the phone book. Stephanie took a deep breath. She'd already practiced her most adult and slightly British-sounding voice. Both Darcy and Allie had said no way did she sound like an eleven-year-old. And so Stephanie dialed the *Dispatch*.

When the operator answered, she asked Stephanie which section of the paper she wished to be connected with.

"Which section?" Stephanie repeated, looking at her notes. "Well, I am calling in reference to the winning stories from the Golden Gate Creative Writing Contest, which your paper plans to print this coming Friday. Perhaps you could tell me which section that might be. Aha, I see.

Local Interest. Yes, please do connect me. And thank you so very, very much."

While she was on hold, Stephanie rolled her eyes at her friends and took a sip of the water that Allie had thought to have at hand.

"Fred Greer, Local Interest," a voice said over the phone.

"Oh, yes, good afternoon, Mr. Greer. I am desper . . . I mean, that is, I am Ms. Desper, an English teacher at John Muir Middle School, and I am calling in reference to the winning stories from the Golden Gate Creative Writing Contest, which your paper plans to print this coming Friday. You see, Mr. Greer, I, and several of the other English teachers from nearby high schools have, of course, read all the winning stories, and we are quite disturbed by one of them, which does not seem to be at all as serious in its subject matter as the other stories. We believe that it makes the contest appear rather *unserious*, if you see what I mean, and I am calling on behalf of hundreds of teachers of English to ask you not to print the winning story from the sixth grade."

Stephanie listened for a moment and then said, "Well, if you must publish *all* the winning stories, couldn't you print the sixth-grade story way in the back? In some section that nobody ever reads? Well, yes, I'm sure all of your sections are very interesting. Ummm. The title? The title of the story that I am calling about is 'No Big Deal.' "

Again Stephanie listened, and she heard Mr. Greer say, " 'No Big Deal'? No, ma'am, I wouldn't kill that story no matter how many English teachers call me up. Why, it's the only piece of writing out of the whole contest that has any real spirit and a genuine voice. No, I certainly won't kill that story, Ms. Desper. But just as you suggested, 'No Big Deal' will appear on a separate page from the other stories."

"Well, that's lovely, just lovely."

"But it won't be buried in the back, no, ma'am. It'll be on page four. It's the very story we're planning to lead off with."

Stephanie forgot about using her grown-up British voice as she said, "I see. Thank you very much for your time," and hung up.

"Bad news, huh?" Darcy asked.

"Well, the good news is that he really liked my story," said Stephanie. Then she added in a glum voice, "The bad news is that not only are they planning to print 'No Big Deal,' but they're printing it first."

That night at dinner, when Stephanie announced that 'No Big Deal' had won first place for sixth grade in the contest, everyone around the Tanner table cheered. Even Nicky and Alex joined in the clapping from their high chairs.

"Why, that's just wonderful!" Danny exclaimed. "My daughter, the writer!"

"My sister, the writer," Michelle echoed.

"Way to go!" said D.J.

"I knew you could do it!" said Becky. "I knew if you just found a subject you cared about, you'd be the big winner."

"By the way," said Jesse, "what did you write about?"

"Oh," said Stephanie, "I guess you could say it's a futuristic story of doomed love."

"Now there's something you know a lot about," said Joey, giving her a puzzled look.

"I must say, Steph," said Danny, "you don't seem as excited as I thought you'd be about winning the contest."

"I'm excited," said Stephanie cheerlessly. "Really excited."

After dinner, Stephanie and D.J. were on do-the-dishes duty again. Stephanie volunteered to do most of the work to make up for the night she'd had her blistered hands all bandaged up, and D.J. accepted the offer.

As she took a seat at the counter to keep her sister company, D.J. said, "You know, I keep running into Eddie in the halls at school, and he keeps giving me these really strange looks. A couple of times, he's even come up and tried to talk to me about that letter I supposedly wrote to him. It's getting embarrassing, Steph, and I'm starting to feel like a real creep."

Stephanie winced. "I know, I know. I should have told him the truth by now, but it just seems so *hard*." She sighed. "I might as well tell him soon, though, because he's going to find out about my big crush on him anyway." And she told D.J. all about how her story was going to be in the paper day after tomorrow. "And," she finished up, "I'm ninety-nine per-cent sure that Eddie will read the winning stories. Then he'll know just exactly how I feel about him."

"I didn't want to tell you this at dinner tonight," said D.J., "because you seemed sort of down about winning the contest and all, but the chances of Eddie reading your story are closer to one hundred percent."

"Couldn't there be just a one percent chance that maybe he wouldn't look for the stories in Friday's paper?"

D.J. shook her head. "I don't think so. Not when the ninth-grade contest winner is the boy-oh-boy next door."

CHAPTER
11

◆ ◀ ◢ ◆

Thursday morning D.J. arranged for Steve to drive Stephanie to school so she could get there extra early. Stephanie went straight to her English classroom, where Mrs. Burns was hard at work, grading papers.

Stephanie knocked on the doorframe. "Mrs. Burns? May I please speak to you?"

"Certainly," said the English teacher. "Come in and take a seat. You're at school very early this morning, aren't you?"

Stephanie nodded. "I came early to talk to you, Mrs. Burns. About my story. Can't you please, please, *please* call the paper and ask them not to put my story in?"

"I'm sure it's too late for that, Stephanie, but if you could tell me why you are so set against your story appearing, perhaps I could help you in another way."

"I just don't think it's good enough," said Stephanie. "Not next to all those, you know, serious stories that the older students wrote."

"Nonsense," said Mrs. Burns. "I can't accept that reason. Your story is very good, and you know it."

"But it isn't about anything important," said Stephanie. "It's just about some twerpy kids who live in the next century."

"But that's exactly what makes your story work," said Mrs. Burns. "The characters are very real, and they're living in a future that some of you may actually face. That's important, isn't it? And not only does it give us something to think about, but it's also told very humorously."

Stephanie knew that none of her arguments were working, so she decided to go for broke. "Mrs. Burns," she said, "what would you say if I told you that I didn't really write this story? That I copied it out of a library book, word for word. That I plagiarized it!"

Mrs. Burns regarded her student for a moment, the expression in her eyes never changing, but Stephanie thought maybe she could see a slight twitching at the corners of her mouth. Finally she spoke. "Stephanie, what you are suggesting is very serious. But if it's true, please tell me who the real author of 'No Big Deal' is."

"It's . . . uh, Stephen King," said Stephanie. "One of his little-known early stories, before he got all, you know, bloody and everything."

Mrs. Burns laughed out loud. "Oh, for goodness' sake, Stephanie. Do you expect me to believe for one minute that someone else wrote 'No Big Deal'? Stephen King indeed! Why, you are the only person in the whole wide world who could have written that particular story, Stephanie Tanner. I don't know why you don't think writing a funny story is every bit as important as writing a serious one, but believe me, it is. People need to laugh. Especially English teachers."

"Thank you, Mrs. Burns," Stephanie said sheepishly, and she walked quietly out of the classroom. She hoped Mrs. Burns wouldn't think too badly of her for hinting that she'd copied her story.

By the time she reached her locker, Stephanie had already redefined her mission. Maybe the *Dispatch* was going to print her story, but that didn't mean Eddie Schwab had to see it. Somehow, some way, she was going to make sure that Eddie Schwab never laid eyes on her story.

It was pitch dark on Friday morning when Stephanie's clock radio began playing "In My Dreams." At first she merely incorporated the song into *her* dreams, but when the song ended and the disc jockey began talking about traffic tie-ups, she sat bolt upright in her bed. The digital glow read 5:07. Quickly she whipped off her blanket, pulled on her jeans and a sweatshirt, and after a fast trip to the bathroom, padded silently down the stairs.

This was the second time in two weeks that Stephanie had been the very first one up in the whole house. It felt sort of nice to be the only one awake in a house full of sleepers. Outside, the dark was just fading to pink in the east. Stephanie paced back and forth in the living room, afraid that if she sat down, her eyes might close and she'd fall asleep. Back and forth, back and forth she walked until she heard

the *thud* of the paper hitting the stoop. Now
. . . action!

As quietly as possible, Stephanie opened the
front door and stepped out into the dawn. Hop-
ping over her family's paper, she dashed across
the yard, straight for the Schwabs' front porch
and their rolled-up copy of the *San Francisco
Dispatch*.

Stephanie kept low. She had to work fast.
What if Eddie suddenly opened his front door,
ready for one of his early morning walks? How
could she explain what she was doing on his
porch? She wouldn't explain. She couldn't. She
just had to act—fast!

Stephanie reached out for the *Dispatch*. Just
then, Max's large furry head pushed out of his
doggie door. Startled, Stephanie drew back.
Half expecting to see Eddie open the front door,
she flattened herself against the house. She
looked down and saw that Max was halfway
out and halfway in the door. He was looking
at her playfully. The dog took two giant steps
forward and emerged from the Schwabs' house.
He padded over to Stephanie.

"Good dog, Max," she whispered, kneeling
down to pet the dog. "Don't bark now, okay?

It's just me, your good old friend Stephanie from next door. Remember? And Comet? Remember your good old friend Comet?"

Max brought his friendly, slobbery face closer to Stephanie's and began licking her hair.

"Yuck, Max," said Stephanie, shielding her head with her hands. Slowly she got up and inched back over to where the newspaper lay. But just as she reached out for it, the big Saint Bernard opened his mouth and grabbed it between his teeth.

"No, Max!" Stephanie whispered. "This isn't a game."

Max looked at her, his tail wagging. He held the paper tightly between his jaws and took a few playful steps away from the door, as if inviting her to chase him.

"Max! Drop it!"

Max dashed down the steps and then back up to the porch again, the paper in his mouth.

"Come on, boy! Give me the paper. Please? I just want to tear out one little page, and then I'll give it right back, I promise."

Evidently Max thought that Stephanie had suggested a new twist to his come-and-get-the-paper game. He crouched down and turned around, facing his doggie door. Lowering his head, he started to go inside, but the paper, held sideways between his jaws, would not fit through the door. Stephanie watched helplessly as Max backed up and tried again. And again.

"Oh, Maxie," crooned Stephanie, still in a whisper. "Give me the paper, baby. Come on, I'll help you."

At last Max turned around to face Stephanie and dropped the paper at her feet. Quickly Stephanie snatched it up. Trying to ignore the slimy Saint Bernard slobber that coated it, she slipped off the rubber band. Then Max lunged for the paper again, and sections scattered everywhere.

Oh, great! thought Stephanie. *Now the paper is going to be totally destroyed!*

Stephanie wished she had a few extra pairs of hands as she tried to grab each part of the paper before Max could sink his teeth into it. She just knew someone was going to open the door of the Schwabs' house any second and catch her.

At last she tugged the Local Interest section away from Max, handing him the Sports Section to destroy instead. She flipped to page four.

Right there, on the page, she saw bold black letters spelling out "No Big Deal." And in smaller letters beneath it, her own name: Stephanie Tanner.

For a moment Stephanie felt proud to see her name in print, but she had no time to dwell on it. Her heart thumping, she opened the paper wider and was happy to find that pages four and five formed a separate page, not attached to the others in the section. Stephanie simply pulled out the page and wadded it up into a ball.

Quickly she folded up the remaining Local Interest section, put all the paper's sections back in order, rolled the newspaper back up, and slipped on the rubber band. Done.

She handed Max one end of the newspaper. Max accepted it happily, and when Stephanie lifted up the flap on his doggie door, he easily ducked down and into his house. He was bringing in the paper.

Letting out the breath that she felt she'd been holding for the last five minutes, Stephanie picked up the little gray ball that was her story and darted home, thinking, *Mission accomplished!*

CHAPTER

12

♦ ◂ ▸ ♦

Picking up the newspaper on her own front steps, Stephanie opened the door and quietly let herself in. She walked into the kitchen and saw that the coffee maker had already started perking the morning's brew. In a matter of minutes, the Tanner house would be bustling with people racing around to start their days.

Stephanie tossed the paper onto the kitchen table and ran upstairs. She needed a shower this morning, that was for sure. But when she got upstairs, she heard the shower already running.

Stephanie cracked the door open. "D.J.?"

"Come on in if you need to!" D.J. called from

inside the shower stall. "I'll be out of here in a minute."

"I can wait!" Stephanie called back. Then she turned on the taps and began soaping all the Saint Bernard slobber off her hands.

As she was washing, another knock sounded at the bathroom door.

"Steph?" came Jesse's voice.

"I'm here!" Stephanie called back.

"Listen, there's a Mrs. Burns on the phone."

"My English teacher?"

"She wants to know if you can be on *Teen Scene*. You have to be at the studio tomorrow morning."

Wow! Stephanie thought. *Teen Scene must want to interview me about my writing!*

"Steph?" Jesse called. "What should I tell her?"

"Tell her okay!" Stephanie shouted through the door.

This was it, she thought. Her big break! With her story safely out of Eddie's newspaper and an interview coming up on a talk show, Stephanie began to feel very good about the way her life was going.

As soon as Stephanie was out of the shower

and dressed, she ran downstairs to get the details about *Teen Scene.*

Joey was sitting at the kitchen counter, reading the paper, while Michelle and D.J. were bustling around getting their breakfasts.

"Hi, Joey," said Stephanie. "Have you seen Jesse?"

"He just left to take Nicky and Alex for their checkups," said Joey. "Say, Steph, congratulations! I'm right in the middle of reading your story. It's great!"

"Yeah, Steph," said D.J. "Nice work!"

"I'm going to read it too," Michelle added. "Joey says it's really funny."

"Thanks," Stephanie said as she poured herself a small bowl of cereal. "Jesse said my English teacher called this morning and asked if I could be on *Teen Scene.* Did he tell you?"

Joey nodded. "That's great," he said. "If you need anyone to stand next to you and do impressions, I volunteer."

"Thanks a lot," said Stephanie, finishing her cereal. "I'll let you know."

"Ready, Steph?" said D.J.

"Ready." Stephanie picked up her backpack and walked out the door with her sister.

At the bus stop, Stephanie told Allie and Darcy all about her call from Mrs. Burns.

"That is so cool," said Darcy.

"Really," said Allie.

"I'm psyched," Stephanie told them. "It probably won't happen, but what if some big publisher is watching, and after the show, I get a call that they want me to write a book and they pay me tons of money for it, so I have to drop out of sixth grade to write full time."

"Sounds good," said Darcy.

"Very good," said Allie.

"And no matter how rich and famous I get, I'll never forget my best friends."

"If you get rich and famous, you'll buy all new clothes, right?" said Allie. "So can I have your white blouse with the rhinestones on the pockets?"

"And I'll take your leather jacket."

"Anything," said Stephanie. "You can have anything you want."

Stephanie had forgotten all about her science assignment to draw a diagram of a water molecule before and after it met a hydrogen molecule, and she barely finished it during science period. Because of this, she arrived late to English class, and she didn't get to speak to Mrs. Burns.

Oh, well, she thought. *I'll talk to her after class.*

Class sped by as Mrs. Burns showed part of a video of *West Side Story* and then led a discussion comparing it to *Romeo and Juliet*. Stephanie became caught up in the tragic story of young love. Talk about a boy-oh-boy next door!

At the end of class Mrs. Burns said, "I hope all of you will tune into *Teen Scene* tomorrow. It's on at noon on channel five," she continued, "and our own Stephanie Tanner will be on the show to read her winning story."

A chorus of oh's, ah's, and wow's filled the classroom.

Stephanie looked puzzled. "I have to read my story out loud?"

"Why, yes," said Mrs. Burns. "What did you think?"

"Well, I . . . I don't know," Stephanie stuttered. "I thought it was more of, you know, more of an interview. More like being on *Oprah* or something."

Mrs. Burns shook her head. "Your time for being on talk shows may come, but for now, please content yourself with appearing on *Teen Scene* to read your story along with the other contest winners. Class dismissed."

Mrs. Burns's students got up from their desks and headed for the door. All except Stephanie. She was too shocked to move. All her work in getting her story out of the Schwabs' paper had been for nothing! All her dreams of becoming a famous writer at the age of eleven were a sham!

"Stephanie?" said Mrs. Burns. "What is it now?"

"Oh, Mrs. Burns," Stephanie said in a voice truly tinged with tragedy, "if I go on that show tomorrow and read my story, the ninth-grade winner will know that I wrote the story about *him*!"

"What if you did write it about him?" Mrs. Burns asked in a voice truly tinged with impatience. "And what if he does realize it? Is this the end of the world?"

"Yes," Stephanie said in a small voice.

Mrs. Burns sighed. "Stephanie, great writers *always* use their friends and relatives as inspiration for their characters. And even if this boy does realize that he is Eduardo, he won't think any less of you. Why, my goodness, Stephanie,

120

he'll be flattered to think that he inspired such a great work of literature."

"Really?" Stephanie blinked back the tears she felt behind her eyes.

"Trust me," said the English teacher. "These things have a way of working out."

CHAPTER
13

◆ ◀ ✦ ◆

Although *Teen Scene* aired at noon on Saturday, the program was taped at 9:00 a.m. The seven contest winners were asked to be on the set by 8:00.

Six of the winning writers milled around on the small TV stage, holding their papers and talking to one another. But the seventh, Stephanie, sat down in a chair opposite her name card and stared into the studio audience in stony silence. Why was it, she wondered, that she was not only the youngest contest winner, but also that she had the only immediate family taking up two entire rows of seats? Not that Darcy and Allie and Steve and Mrs. Burns really counted as immediate family. And no way was Kimmy related. But still, there they all were. And Joey, too, making faces and dying, she knew, to come up on stage himself and do a few impersonations.

As she waited for the taping to begin, Stephanie's eyes occasionally flicked over to Eddie. He was wearing the same red-and-black plaid shirt that he'd had on that first day she'd seen him from her living-room window. He stood now with two other contest winners. Girl winners. They were talking to him in an animated way, their hands gesturing in the air, their heads tilting, their hair swaying. Was it just her imagination or did Eddie look sort of trapped between those two girls? As if he'd really like to excuse himself and come over and talk to her? Of course it was her imagination! And besides, Eddie Schwab was the last person in the whole wide world she wanted to talk to.

"All right, kids, find your name cards on the table and sit down, please," said the producer at last.

Some geeky seventh-grade boy sat down next to Stephanie, and one of the girls who'd been talking to Eddie sat next to the boy. Then came

Eddie. *At least,* Stephanie thought, *he won't be able to look at me while I'm reading my story.*

Things began to happen very quickly then. The producer gave them some tips about licking their lips and looking into the camera from time to time, and then he introduced them to the program's host, Rick Lombardo, who was an old guy, probably in his forties, with thinning hair but dressed in jeans and a T-shirt as if he were still a teenager.

"All *right,*" said Rick. "Let's get the show on the road." He consulted some program notes that he held and then looked up at Stephanie. *"You!"* he said, pointing at her. "You will read first."

Stephanie nodded. At least she'd get it over with. Oh, why had she given her characters such obvious names?

"And *you!*" Now Rick pointed to the seventh-grade boy sitting next to Stephanie. "You'll read next. And so it goes, down the line and working up to the twelfth-grade story. Okay, everybody?"

The producer started counting backward from seven, the studio lights flashed up to their brightest, and at the count of *one,* the camera started rolling.

"Good afternoon," said Rick, "and welcome to *Teen Scene*, the what's-happenin' show for today's teens."

Stephanie tuned out the patter and jumped slightly with surprise when she heard Rick say her name and ". . . reading her winning story, 'No Big Deal.' "

Suddenly an even brighter light focused on Stephanie. She cleared her throat, looked into the camera for a moment the way the producer had asked them to, and in a slightly quavery voice started reading.

Stephana sat in front of her video-imaging mirror, trying to decide just what hairstyle to wear to the spaceship race today. She hit button number 1. Her face remained the way it always was—her high forehead, large violet eyes, slightly turned-up nose never changed—but the imager now showed her long, honey-colored hair combed high on top of her head. Beneath her image appeared the description of the do: THE BEEHIVE.

It was sort of a weird style, from the 1950s, over one hundred years ago. But still, it was amusing. And it made her look older, which, after all, was the point. Now perhaps Eduardo would pay attention to her. Now perhaps he would understand that the three-year difference in their ages was nothing to be concerned about. Was, in fact, no big deal.

Stephanie's voice lost its quaver as she read and as the people in the audience began to chuckle when Stephana's video-imaging mirror reached out with its octopus arms and began styling her hair. By the time she came to the end of "No Big Deal," the audience was laughing at just about everything she said and Stephanie was having the time of her life.

When she finished, Stephanie kept her eyes down on her paper. Eddie *had* to know the story was about him, didn't he? And if she looked up, she might catch him looking right at her. That would be too embarrassing! So she simply looked at her story until Rick began introducing the boy next to her and he started reading his story, titled "Have Bike, Will Recyc." From what she could comprehend, it was about a group of boys who formed an after-school recycling club.

Now Stephanie's nervousness came back. The palms of her hands felt wet and clammy. Her forehead, too. And her heart was still beating as if she'd just run a long race. She tried to listen to the boy's story, but her attention wavered. And when the eighth-grade girl began reading her story about the long and painful death of a sewer rat caused by his toxic environment, Stephanie stopped even trying to listen and simply let her mind wander.

Now it was Eddie's turn. Stephanie's heart began to beat even faster. She snuck a peek at him as he read his title, "A Brand-New World." Thinking that his winning entry would no doubt be about some important news event from the other side of the globe or a catalog of ways to save the planet, she was surprised when the piece turned out to be a science-fiction story about Jeddo, a shy young Earthling whose single-occupant spacecraft becomes separated from the rest of its convoy. When Jeddo makes an emergency landing on the planet Friscodonia, his spacecraft is destroyed and, with no chance of being rescued, he must remain the only Earthling in Friscodonia. The Friscodonians are friendly, but so different from Jeddo, with their many eyes that protrude on stems from all parts of their bodies. Jeddo feels terribly alone until Zonka, a six-eyed Friscodonian girl, befriends him. As time goes by, Zonka makes life on the alien planet feel less and less weird, and it is she who notices that right in the middle of his forehead he is beginning to grow a third eye himself as he becomes more and more used to living in a brand-new world.

As the other students read their work, Stephanie could hardly get over her surprise about Eddie's story. It wasn't like the others at all—grim and depressing. It was really interesting and suspenseful. A good story.

Finally the *Teen Scene* host looked into the camera's eye and said, "This is Rick Lombardo for *Teen Scene*. See you next Saturday." And it was over.

Stephanie stood up and walked as quickly as she could toward the greenroom, where the producer had told them that their families would meet them after the show.

"Stephanie!" Eddie called after her. "Wait a second!"

Caught between wanting to stop and wanting to break into a run, Stephanie did both. First she sped up, but then, right inside the green-room, she stopped and turned around. What point was there in trying to avoid the boy next door forever? Better get the embarrassment over with now.

"Hi, Eddie," said Stephanie as two other story winners squeezed past her to get into the room.

"I just wanted to tell you how much I liked your story," said Eddie, walking over to her. "It was really funny, all that stuff about the video mirror. Where'd you ever come up with an idea like that?"

"Oh, I don't know," said Stephanie, hardly noticing all the story winners milling around the room. "Maybe it was inspired by that scene in *Snow White*—you know, where the wicked stepmother is sitting in front of her mirror?"

Eddie laughed. "I can see that," he said, and then he looked puzzled. "You know, it was really strange. I'd read all the other stories that were on the show today in yesterday's paper. Except for yours."

"Really?" Stephanie gulped. "That *is* strange."

"I think I know what happened, though."

"You do?"

"Yeah. Max tries to bring our paper in every morning like he used to do in L.A., where we had a wider doggie door, but he can't quite do it and the paper ends up wrecked. You should have seen our paper yesterday. What a mess." Eddie shook his head. "Or maybe he just liked your story so much he ate it up."

Now Stephanie laughed. It felt so good to be talking to Eddie again. "Well," she said, "I'm sort of embarrassed that you had to hear my story, because I guess . . . well, you probably know that you sort of inspired it." And while she was confessing, she thought, she might as well do it up right. So she made herself keep going. "I had such a big crush on you when you first moved in that . . . well, maybe you've already figured this out, but I was the one who wrote you the letter you found in your locker, not D.J."

Eddie gave Stephanie a startled look. "Oh, that explains a lot of things, like why D.J.'s been avoiding me ever since that day." He was quiet for a minute. Stephanie noticed that most of the other story winners had already gathered up their things and were leaving.

"Well," Eddie went on, "you're not embarrassed anymore about putting me in your story, are you? After all, I did the same to you."

"Huh?" said Stephanie. "Hey, wait a second, you mean Zonka, the six-eyed alien girl, is supposed to be *me*?"

"I never reveal my sources," said Eddie, laughing. "I just wish I could write a story as funny as yours."

"That's weird," said Stephanie. "Because . . ."

"Because what?"

"Well," said Stephanie, "I don't know, I just thought, knowing you a little, that your story would be about something like not using gas-powered lawn mowers or being a vegetarian or something . . ."

"Something earth-shatteringly important?"

Stephanie nodded.

Eddie shrugged. "I guess you don't know me as well as you thought you did." He paused, and then added, "Maybe, since I'd just moved here and everything, I was feeling insecure, so I overdid the environmental stuff. You know, to impress you."

Impress me? Stephanie thought. *Amazing!* And now that she knew that she and Eddie had, for a little while at least, been trying to impress each other, she felt better. Now she was willing to let the boy-oh-boy next door be, well, just a boy. Just a friend. And who knew? Maybe if she ever lived to be 122 and Eddie lived to be 125 . . .

"Hey, Steph!" yelled Joey as he and the rest of her family began crowding into the green-room. "You were the best, baby!"

"Really," said D.J., giving her sister a hug. "This story was even funnier than 'The San Francisco Pickle Emergency.' "

"The *what* emergency?" said Eddie.

D.J. turned and looked at Eddie uncomfortably. "Uh, pickle," she said.

"Relax, D.J.," said Stephanie. "I've confessed. Eddie now knows who really wrote the letter."

D.J. smiled, obviously relieved. "But did you confess that you write stories with titles like 'The San Francisco Pickle Emergency'?"

Eddie laughed. "She didn't," he said, "but somehow I'm not all that surprised."

"Okay, now you *really* know everything," said Stephanie. "I have nothing left to confess."

Stephanie saw then that Eddie's parents had

come into the greenroom too. They were talking and laughing with Danny and Joey and Jesse and Becky.

"Say, everybody," Danny said, "let's get going before the producer kicks us out of here." He turned to Eddie's parents. "What do you folks say to coming over to our house for lunch to celebrate the successful TV appearances of Eddie Schwab and Stephanie Tanner?"

Art Schwab looked at his wife.

Joyce nodded. "What a nice idea. We'd love to."

"Great," said Joey. "I've got a batch of my special vegetarian chili simmering on the stove right this moment. Come on, Steph, Eddie, you two TV stars ride home with me and Michelle."

As they headed out to the parking lot, Stephanie turned to Eddie. "I do have just one more thing to confess," she said.

"Let me guess," said Eddie. "Is it that your vegetarian chili is pretty similar to Joey's recipe?"

Stephanie nodded and climbed into the backseat of Joey's car. "I *did* invent the taco-shell topping, but it's Joey's chili."

"I'm so hungry right now," said Eddie, climbing in after her and shutting the door, "that I don't care if it's Comet's chili recipe."

"Okay," said Joey as he started up the engine. "See, there was this man who took his dog, Fido, to the movie, and at every really funny part throughout the whole movie, Fido laughed and laughed. . . ."

While Joey's voice droned on and on in the front seat, Stephanie turned to Eddie in the back. "Just think," the girl next door whispered to the boy next door, "if you live to be one hundred and twenty-two and I live to be one hundred and twenty-five . . ."

"Just think what?" Eddie whispered back.

"Just think," said Stephanie, "how many times we might have to listen to this joke!"

An all-new series of novels based on your
favorite character from the hit TV series!

FULL HOUSE™
Stephanie

Phone Call From a Flamingo

Stephanie is excited to join the most popular club in school,
but are the Flamingoes a cool club or bad news?

The Boy-Oh-Boy Next Door

He's the cutest boy she's ever seen...but when her secret crush
becomes front page news, Stephanie wishes she'd never laid
eyes on the new kid on the block!

Twin Troubles

Stephanie is in charge of the sixth grade carnival and she has to
baby-sit the twins. Will Stephanie's first job be a double disaster?

Hip Hop Till You Drop

The Flamingoes are out to win the talent show.
How far will Stephanie go to stop them?
(Available mid-March 1994)

Don't miss any of Stephanie's new adventures!

Available from Minstrel® Books
Published by Pocket Books

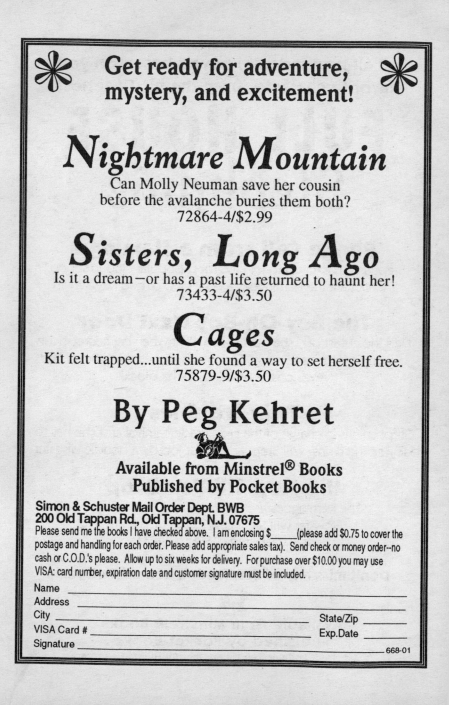

Get ready for adventure, mystery, and excitement!

Nightmare Mountain
Can Molly Neuman save her cousin
before the avalanche buries them both?
72864-4/$2.99

Sisters, Long Ago
Is it a dream—or has a past life returned to haunt her!
73433-4/$3.50

Cages
Kit felt trapped...until she found a way to set herself free.
75879-9/$3.50

By Peg Kehret

Available from Minstrel® Books
Published by Pocket Books